# LIFE is TRICHY

Memoir of a mental health therapist
with a mental health disorder

Lindsey M. Muller

For information about this title, to order other books and/or
electronic media, or for press inquiry, contact the publisher:

Mindful Publishing Co.
P.O. Box 35852 Los Angeles, CA. 90035
www.lifeistrichy.com
lifeistrichybook@gmail.com

ISBN: 978-0-692-32244-4 (Paperback)
       978-0-692-32245-1 (Electronic)
Printed in the United States of America

For therapy inquiry in the Los Angeles area, contact the author:
www.lmullertherapy.com
lmullertherapy@gmail.com

Cover and Interior Design:
Copyright © 2014
DesignsDoneNow.com

Author Photo:
Copyright © 2014 Sam Schneider Photography.

This book is nonfiction.

Names have been changed or shortened to protect

the privacy of the individuals involved,

but that does not in any way alter the facts.

To all those who are struggling to understand
and prevail in this trichy life.

# Table of Contents

# Acknowledgments

To my parents, who stayed positive, supportive, and inquisitive through my various challenges. They never gave up on the mental health system or me, and actively pursued answers. I can never thank you enough for your unconditional love, support, and acceptance. You have taught me that hard work can accomplish dreams.

To my younger brothers, two of my best friends, who stood by and witnessed my challenges as they unfolded even if they did not quite understand. Thank you for supporting me with this endeavor and everything else I have pursued.

To my grandparents, aunts, uncles, and cousins who are great sources of support to me, always with my best interest at heart. I love you all. You have taught me that family is everything.

To Stephanie, the sister I never had, who is one of my biggest fans and emotional outlets. Thank you for your encouragement during the writing process. This book is as much your story as it is my story. Here's to us, and our beautiful futures with gorgeous hair.

To JP, for your love, support, inquisitive nature, and insight. You asked a lot of great questions to help channel my thoughts for the writing process. Thank you for backing my ideas and for accepting me. Thank you for your help with my website and marketing.

To Lisa Knight, Sally Naylor, and Lindsay Marder for your interest in my story, and for turning my thoughts into a beautiful image and colorful prose. Thank you for dedicating your time and effort. Without the three of you, my words would not fit beautifully into a book.

To every professor and teacher who was a part of my incredible education. My knowledge came from you, as well as life, and together I was able to piece things together and make sense of my life.

To Jessica, and the incredible team at *Thursday's*, thank you for your expertise in color, cuts, and hair attachments. You always make me look and feel like a celebrity. My hair has never looked better.

To Juliette Bennett, a talented makeup artist, and Sam Schneider, a dynamite photographer. Thank you for helping me look gorgeous during my back cover photo shoot. May you both have continued success.

Most importantly to God, I thank Him for giving me life. Although at times I felt less than thankful, I can't help but give the glory to him for all I have accomplished and who I have become.

# Preface

Our society is fascinated by real life situations. Look around: *People* magazine, *US Weekly* magazine, sports documentaries, the biography section at your local bookstore, reality television. Movies mirror real life, which is why actors work so hard to appear as natural as possible. We naturally take interest in these shows, books, movies, and magazines. Why? It is a source of entertainment but also a source of comfort. We all have our struggles, challenges, and weaknesses, and it is comforting to meet another person who is willing to admit to her problems and share her story. When you hear of another's struggle, you do not feel as distant. Suddenly, this raw and vulnerable individual increases in value and worth. Why? Because from experience comes knowledge and empathy. After all, why would we go through so many hardships if nothing positive resulted? *Everything happens for a reason.* I believe this to be true.

For ten years I entertained the idea of writing a book about my journey and never told anyone I was considering it. I was undecided and did not want the influences of others to be the determining factor. I knew that if I were to release my memoir to the public, I would undoubtedly be known as *that woman with that strange disorder.* Unfortunately that is a downside to mental health diagnosis. It is called labeling. Did I really want the stigma? Conversely, I felt that I owed it to everyone struggling to know that I, too, was at one time or another in that same place in life. I found a way to persevere and emerge victorious. There is something to be said for overcoming the hardships which life serves us. I thought that perhaps by sharing my story I could instill hope in those finding their way through Trichotillomania, or any other challenge.

After weighing positives and negatives, I made my decision. With butterflies in my stomach, I sat down to write. I dismissed the notion that I would be identified by just my disorder, as this is far from the truth in the grand scheme of life (as you will see). The overall vision was, and still is, that this book would serve many purposes and help many.

There are not many books written about this disorder and of those published, none are like this. Here you will gain the perspective of one individual who describes what it is like to have a mental health disorder while attempting to live like everyone else. Unlike other books that share a story of a mental or physical challenge, I also have the professional and psychological knowledge of many years of formal education to share, in an attempt to demystify the thoughts and emotions behind the disorder.

I have been both the clinician and the patient. I do not claim to have it all figured out, nor do I believe that my experience is like everyone else's who may have been diagnosed with the same disorder. This could not be further from the truth. However, we learn more from research and listening to those who are willing to share their experience, for no two stories are the same.

I started writing with a mix of emotions. Being a perfectionist in my work among other areas of my life, I was concerned that this book would not be a success, would not clearly articulate its purpose, and would not find its proper place on the shelves among the plethora of psychology or self-help memoirs or texts. Further, while I have an extensive education and have written countless graduate papers, I have never attempted to write a book. However, I know that anyone with a purpose, a passion, and a story can write if he or she takes the time.

Many decisions go into writing a book. Where do I begin? How much detail do I include before it borders on boredom or presents only superfluous information? Do I write from my professional voice or from a patient's perspective? Who is my target audience? What constitutes an ending, and what exactly would be a good ending? I realized that the writing process is a good metaphor for life. Sometimes you just need to take a leap of faith and let things unravel as they may, or figure it out as you go. This was my approach when delving into the uncharted territory of the writing world.

You may be the parent of a child who is trying to understand and find answers or you may be the one that is struggling. Perhaps you are a spouse and just want to understand. Or, you may be a medical professional who wants clarity about what may be happening in the mind of your patient from another medical professional's (and patient's) perspective. You may be none of these—merely an inquisitive individual who has an interest in real life struggles and victories.

Whoever you are, I thank you for finding this book. I am confident that you will gain something from your reading, whether it is knowledge, comfort, hope, motivation, and understanding, or just diversion. I have taken a risk, and decided to shove the perfect portrayal of myself to the side, a portrayal I had for so long tried to uphold, but have now exchanged for the truth. Welcome to my story, my journey, and my life with Trichotillomania.

—Lindsey Marie Muller

PART 1
# THE BEGINNING

# 1

September 22. My parent's lives were forever changed. Not only did they become first-time parents, their learning process was expedited. For my mom, this meant lots of matching outfits, which included shoes, hair bows, and jewelry. For my dad, this meant utter joy and love. I was daddy's little girl. They were obsessed and so in love with their little girl.

"Hey darling, what do you think Lindsey will be like at five?"

Mom replied, "I have no idea, but I cannot wait. I look forward to the day she takes her first step, so we can enroll her in dance class. I have a lavender ballerina tutu already hanging in her closet."

My parents were the best I could have wanted. Every day was full of fun, excitement, laughs, and learning. They wanted to teach me as much as they could, as fast as they could. I would spend hours doing workbooks and watching educational programs: *Sesame Street, Mr. Roger's Neighborhood,* and *Reading Rainbow.*

"Lindsey, what do you want to do once we are finished baking cookies?"

"Another workbook. I like learning. Am I getting smart?" I was well on my way to becoming a scholar at two-year's-old.

Being of a scholastic mindset, I have often wondered why it

is that almost any tangible item involving more than a single step comes with a manual or guide; yet, probably the hardest job ever, parenting, is just one of those trial-and-error, fly-by-the-seat-of-your-pants, experiences that last a lifetime. I have pondered what it would be like if parents were given a three thousand page manual with a *Frequently Asked Questions* section. Wouldn't that be nice! In fact, three thousand pages do not seem like enough, for no two children are the same and no two lives are the same. The parent-child dynamic is forever evolving and adapting. Each time you parent a new child, you are doing it all over again for the first time. No two days with the same child will ever be the same, for each day you, the parent, are one day wiser and one day more experienced. On the day you may think you finally have it all figured out and have mastered the art of parenting, a curve ball is thrown. Even if there were a manual, it would only help to an extent because parents have emotions too. The manual may provide information about working through a situation that is observable, but there is no indication of what emotions are elicited as a result of living through that moment. Despite the realities of parenting, my parents sure did a great job, and still are doing a great job. Parenting is truly intangible and immeasurable.

I attended two years of preschool at an idyllic small Christian school before it was decided where I would attend elementary school. I clearly remember the day my kindergarten teacher came to the house for the first time. At my school, the kindergarten teachers would come to each child's house for *Meet-Your-Teacher Day* in preparation for the upcoming school year. This was an opportunity for the teacher to see where the child lived and for the parents to prepare drinks and snacks to share with the teacher while they discussed their son or daughter's developmental milestones. Enter here: parental bragging rights.

"Lindsey, let's get you dressed. Your new teacher will be here soon." My mother had planned my outfit for the special occasion; a frilly *Guess* jean skirt, a white ruffle-sleeved top, white lace socks, red *Mary Jane* shoes, and an oversized red bow.

"Thank you for picking this one, Mommy. This is one of my favorite outfits." If it were not for the perfectly matched outfit, I would not have been in such a happy mood that day. I always wanted to appear meticulous.

Miss Anderson was sitting with my parents as they discussed how ahead of the curve I was in comparison to my classmates.

"Yes, Miss Anderson, Lindsey is already reading entire books," my mother confidently remarked.

"Miss..Miss..Miss Anderson, do you want to see me read?" I stuttered from excitement. Before I could hear the answer, I was already in front of my gray and white bookshelf, which matched my height. *Goodnight Moon, Curious George, One Fish Two Fish, Green Eggs and Ham*…decisions, decisions.

"Here…here it is. Listen to me read *Go Dog Go.*" As I raced back to the table where my parents and Miss Anderson sat, I frantically waved the book in the air.

I read the entire book cover to cover. To this day, I am still proud of my early phonetic skill development. And so, my kindergarten year was often spent reading to the rest of the class during the regularly scheduled *reading circle.*

It was easy to observe my fully developed personality from a young age. Developmental psychologists like to debate as to what age a child develops a personality. Psychological jargon refers to *the time before identifiable personality* as temperament, or emotional reactions to environment that one is born with, which later emerge into a personality. In my case, who I am today is exactly who I was at age three. I had a rather socially interactive childhood with lots of play-dates and sleepovers. What this meant for me, even as a preschooler, was:

1) I would always get overwhelmed if there were too many toys taken out at once.

2) I would boss my friend(s) to put everything away in its exact place before taking out the next toy.

3) I was the leader and controlled what the rules were and who played what role during make-believe play time.

4) I was much more verbose and intuitive than my playmates.

5) When I was tired of the play-date I moved on, and it was time for my friend to leave whether they were ready to go or not.

6) I often put more mental energy into making sure everyone was playing correctly (telling who to do what) than into just having fun.

7) If I was not good at something or better than everyone else, I discredited the activity; and...

8) There better not have been visitors unless I was *dressed to the nines* and pleased with my outfit.

Basically, what all of this translates to, in adult personality terminology, is a perfectionistic, type-A personality.

My first brother was born when I was two. My second brother was born when I was five. I was so in love with both of them. I don't know whether I was happier to have a new little person to play with or a new brother to boss. Either way, I spent a lot of time interacting with them, teaching them, hugging, kissing and squeezing them, and being a second mother. I thought that as the older sister it was my job to be the eyes and ears for my mom when she couldn't be everywhere all the time. I would excitedly tell her when one of my brothers did something new or amazing, and would make sure she scolded them a second time (after I had) if they did something wrong. I fulfilled my big sister role to the utmost of my ability, and I was good at it. My brothers loved me and looked up to me, and I loved them too. I developed different relationships with each of them, and to this day, they are my best friends.

Childhood was an amazing time. My brothers and I played sports and engaged in many hobbies. We would take family trips and summer adventures. We had the best birthday parties (more like week-long birthday celebrations) and family gatherings with all of my relatives. My mom was a great cook. My dad was always goofing around with us. My parents were there for protection, guidance, and as a solid sounding board. They worked together as a great team and shared the disciplinarian responsibilities. We had amazing family pets and countless toys. We attended the best private schools and were constantly challenged. We were taught to work hard and understand the value of money. We were socially adjusted and well mannered. My mother always dressed us commendably, and we took pride in good grooming habits. My hair was always styled with bows, hats, headbands, barrettes, or curls. One of the most relaxing times was when my mother would sit on the floor, I in her lap, while she brushed my thick, chocolate-colored hair with natural streaks of golden. I was known for having incredibly thick hair. It was not long before my parents were calling me *Hair Bear*.

In speaking with my brothers, they agreed without reservation that the environment we grew up in was one of enrichment and nurturance. By no means am I implying that my home was perfect for there is no such thing. But, the imperfections in my home life were perfect in their own way. We had our usual spats, yelling at one another. I was caught lying a few times. I was grounded once or twice. And I did not always agree with my parent's ways or get along with my brothers. That was acceptable. As far as I am concerned, this was all typical, healthy family *stuff*.

# 2

When there is an illness or an accident, the most commonly asked questions to the attending doctor are typically either *how did this happen* or *what caused this*. Somehow it seems that if we know the underlying cause it makes everything more tolerable. I took the time to describe my childhood in an attempt to show that mental *dis-order* can grow from *order*. Whether a person struggles with diabetes or anxiety, for example, does not imply fault. This is an important point. Yes, certain mental disorders may arise from childhood maltreatment or stressors, but one does not cause the other in all cases. A child who has never experienced a trauma can present for treatment of Generalized Anxiety Disorder just like a child who *has* experienced a trauma. Also, mental disorders do not emerge from a child viewing her childhood as awful and miserable. Many happy children never come in contact with a mental health treatment provider or disorder but others, like me, do.

Clients often ask me, "Miss Muller, where did we screw up? What did we do wrong? We tried to be the best parents, and it still was not good enough."

The only thing more upsetting than this is when parents assume the worst, like their child experienced an intense traumatic event that has remained a secret from them for years and years. I am a living testament to the contrary. I neither endured a traumatic event nor held secrets as to why I developed behavioral habits. You will soon learn of the precipitating event, which was anything but traumatic. If anything, it was just unusual.

Mental health disorders often hold a negative connotation because they can come across as perplexing and frightening. One day, little Jane suddenly develops a rash, hives, and swelling. Over time, she becomes frightened and complains that she is having a hard time swallowing and breathing. Jane's mom takes her to the pediatrician where the doctor provides a verbal assessment, or runs through a list of questions, to determine exactly what is and is not going wrong. While a rash can develop for many reasons, and breathing difficulty can be caused by many other issues, these symptoms all presenting in the same person fall into the category and diagnosis of food allergy.

At some point, Jane developed a food allergy to corn. Was she born with it? Maybe or maybe not. Is the allergy due to an overexposure to the allergen? Likely. Is Jane's food allergy due to her parent's lack of dietary monitoring? No. Jane has been told she has a food allergy. She will have to take the proper precautions to keep the symptoms minimized. The food allergy is a microscopic part of Jane's whole life. The person, known as Jane, is made up of more than her food allergy. Jane's parents are also identified as greater than their daughter's current food allergy. This may seem like a rather rudimentary example but mental health issues are very much the same.

# 3

As young as I can remember, I had hair issues. By hair issues, I mean hairstyle issues.

I am standing in front of my bedroom mirror as my hair rests on my shoulders. My hands are sticky from the excessive amount of gel and hairspray, which has formed a crusty paste on my palms. My shoulders ache from holding my arms to my head in tough attempt to secure my hair in a smooth ponytail with a scrunchie. This is my *go-to look*; a slicked back ponytail without bumps. My temples are pulsing violently as I try over and over to pull my hair back tighter and tighter. God help me if I see one slight bump; I will start all over. This is my unspoken but always implemented rule.

This perpetual desire to have the perfect ponytail often led to anger. I can still recall the feeling of annoyance bordering on a blood-boiling anger because my hair was not doing the right thing. It was just that important. If my hair had bumps, it was a hard sell to get me into the car for school. This just meant I was sometimes in a rush to get to school on time.

"Gosh, hair, why won't you just do what I want you to do?"

It was almost as if my hair was defying me and had taken on a life of its own. My hair knew how I wanted it to look, but it would not cooperate. Some mornings my mom would do my hair for me to try to prevent this entire experience from unraveling as it did many mornings. Instead of being a deterrent, I would displace my frustration at her and think that she couldn't do my hair right either. My mood was determined by my hair and to a larger extent by my appearance. I was in second grade.

I was identifying my sense of worth and sense of self from my external appearance. If my hair had bumps, I did not like myself because all my classmates would look at the bumps and cast judgment. Somehow, my hairstyle was the deciding factor in how I felt about myself and what everyone else thought of me that day. According to Jean Piaget, a Swiss Developmental Psychologist, *egocentrism* is a normal part of development. While I was always identified as being advanced and mature for my age, certain aspects of my development were on point, and some were somewhat regressive. To explain Piaget's concept in one sentence, preschoolers' thinking abilities are limited by egocentrism, or the inability to distinguish one's own point of view from the viewpoint of others. So in this case, since I was so focused on my hair, I believed everyone else was too. Egocentrism takes

on a similar form in teenage years, so I prefer to think of my cognitive development as advanced rather than immature.

Adolescent egocentrism is typical of the developmental process as well. In psychology, we see the repetition of self-focus when one thinks that everyone else is focusing on just her behavior and appearance. As discussed by psychologist

David Elkind, the associated beliefs are the *personal fable*, or the concept that teens believe themselves to be unique and special ("No one else can understand what I am going through"), and the *imaginary audience*, or the concept that one's behavior or appearance is magnified in everyone else's eyes ("Every student is going to focus in on this bump in my hair"). These two concepts highlight my second grade thought process. In hindsight, I was also able to identify the pressure I put on myself to look and act like an adult from a young age, which was likely due to two reasons. One, I frequently heard I was so advanced and mature from the adults around me, and two, I embraced the second mother role to my brothers from a young age. Maybe I envisioned leaving the house with an *unpolished* hairdo as something only acceptable to children, and despite my chronological age, that clearly was not me as far as I was concerned. For those who may be wondering, egocentrism has a flavor of narcissism.

While I placed so much emphasis on my hair and clothing presentation (despite wearing school uniforms for the majority of my grade school years), my appearance became my greatest weakness. I was something of a mystery.

*Body focused repetitive behaviors (BFRB's)* is a name given to a group of behaviors involving one or more actions done to one's own body over and over, ultimately leading to immense physical and emotional damage. I began my first *BFRB* in kindergarten in the form of skin picking. Nail biting followed. Then, both behaviors occurred simultaneously. The nail biting was more acceptable and understood given that immediate family members did the same. The skin picking was a whole different monster, one that warranted immediate professional attention and advice.

# 4

Unfortunately I do not remember the exact day when I started skin picking and nail biting, but I know I was in kindergarten when I first discovered another one of my favorite activities, along with dancing and Brownies. I have often wondered how I knew to self-mutilate. I had not learned the picking and biting from anyone I had ever been around, and surely, this was not something I saw modeled on *Sesame Street*.

I picked at my arms and legs. To clarify, I did not scratch or pick at something that was not there. I primarily focused on ant bites or mosquito bites, which formed semi-regularly from being at the ball ground or park. The bite would start as merely a miniscule bite; yet, once I got my hands on it, I could easily make it something more. The bites became a playground for exploration and something that I had with me at all times. Although my nails were always bitten down to the skin, I found a way to pick. I was a determined young skin picker.

Skin picking included two activities. The first was actually digging my semblance of a nail under the scab (if the scab was hard enough) and pulling it away so a round, open area was exposed. Then I would squeeze, much like some adults squeeze pimples. If the scab were somewhat soft, I would go right to squeezing. In describing, this may seem like it takes time, focus, and that I was inflicting pain, but this was not my experience.

The interesting thing about BFRB's is that some occur in awareness as a conscious choice, and some are done almost to pass the time. I will explain more about this later. The scab squeezing was really my go to activity, and I thought I was smart about it. While sitting in the backseat of my mother's or father's car, I would choose the seat right behind the driver, so I would not get caught. I clearly remember my exact thought process. I would spend considerable time looking and looking for my next target.

With recurrence, many of my scabs became infected, and I knew this from one of three ways; a red ring, a strong pulsating charge, or a swollen raised area. That added another level of fun and curiosity as I was never sure whether squeezing would result in red blood or yellow-white pus indicative of infection. There was no pain in any of this. Next, I would either pull up my scrunch sock (the popular socks of the 80's) and use it to dab the blood or pus or I would get a tissue and put the corner of the tissue into the extraction to watch how it diffused the tissue a new color. I picked and bit whenever I felt like it for my habits were never persnickety. It did not matter whether I was in school, at a birthday party, or with my parents. If I did pick my skin or bite my nails before my parents, it resulted in a rather dull consequence usually in the form of being told to stop or making a big deal about how awful my arms and legs looked.

What could they really do? I was rather resistant to my parent's interventional tactics.

Despite my smarts, I was never able to step back, look at my arms and legs, and decide for myself that it looked awful (almost bordering on diseased, to be frank). All I focused on, if anything, was the enjoyment in completion of the activity. For me, these behaviors were a way to fill time when I was bored. Boredom. That was my emotion. I do not mean that I was necessarily mentally bored, for I would even pick my skin or bite my nails while I was sitting in class learning. It was boredom from sensory deprivation.

I was intuitive enough to recognize that the times I did not pick or bite were when I received adequate sensory stimulation. Sensory stimulation is adequately using one or more of the senses; touch, sight, smell, taste, sound. Eating a meal, playing a sport, dancing, taking a shower, swimming, listening to music and brushing my teeth were all free from *BFRB*'s. Aside from these times, I think I was always going after one of the two behaviors, gnawing at my nails or hacking away at my arms and legs. My in-depth description of how these behaviors looked, when they happened, and how I accomplished doing what I did, may lead many to question why. My educated guess is that the behaviors stemmed from boredom or sensory deprivation. However, this information does not correct anything.

My parents were devastated in seeing such a beautiful little girl destroy her skin. They often told me:

"You can only cover this for so long unless you plan to be wearing pants and long sleeves in the middle of the Florida summer. Do you want to grow up and have scars all over your body as an adult? What do you think will happen when you get older and you have a boyfriend? He will say 'Ew, Lindsey, what happened to you? Are you contagious?' Your scars cannot be fixed. You are only given one body, and you are ruining a beautiful girl."

As parents, this was undoubtedly upsetting and preposterous behavior. Despite having two other children to care for, my mother and father equally spent a lot of time trying to find answers and prevent me from ruining myself. I wish I had been able to listen to what they were telling me. I wish the words had been strong motivation to cut right through my habitual drive and stop me. In fact, I wish I had never started. But I did, and this was my reality for several years.

The first line of defense was my amazing pediatrician. He remained our pediatrician until the day came that our bodies physically could not fit on the examination table.

"Why are you doing this to yourself? You are such a beautiful and smart little girl," Dr. P inquired.

Truth be told, I had no honest answer. I certainly did not want to do this to myself, yet I never really had the motivation to stop.

The most understandable parallel is when one decides to diet. How many times have you, or perhaps someone you know, spoken of wanting to lose weight and needing to diet? The first step is to devise a plan to either eliminate certain food groups such as fats, meat, sugar, or carbohydrates, or to decide to simply reduce calories. The large family party consisting of six courses and alcoholic beverages creeps onto your calendar, and on that very evening you are faced with a decision. Do you stick to the diet or deviate just for the festivities? In compromise, you decide that you will have just one bite of dessert. That is fair. However, when you actually get down to noshing, one bite turns into two and you think to yourself, "I certainly do not want to set myself back and do this to myself." At the conclusion of the evening, the delectable morsels of goodness win. The conscious or unconscious decision to finish off the entire dessert emerged victorious over your thoughts and motivation as you leave the restaurant with a satiated belly of sugar. At that point, you realize how awful you feel physically because your blood sugar is through the roof, and psychologically for losing behavioral control. A common thought follows. "There is always tomorrow to buckle down and get back to my dieting goal."

Dieting, or lack thereof, parallels my behavioral experience. I did not like how my arms and legs looked, but I did it anyway. I did not want to negatively impact those around me by engaging in such behavior, but I did. I also knew in the back of my mind that if I were to make the decision to try to stop, there was always tomorrow. And at the end, there remained two questions: Why does this happen, and what is the treatment plan?

Dr. P, endorsing all things pediatric, gave his response from his pediatric-filtered lens; a response that is all too common among pediatricians but certainly not wrong in any way. To answer the question of why I did what I did, he explained that it had to do with hormonal changes (i.e. development and growth spurts) and the underlying (unconscious) anxiety of those changes. The treatment plan was that I would grow out of it, essentially growing tired of the picking and nail biting, and one day I would just stop. When questioned by my parents, he said that they were more than welcome to take me to a child psychologist if they so desired, but in time I would stop anyway. I presume this was great news to my parents as it meant that this was not a long-lasting disorder. It, however, was not a guarantee because some individuals do continue to pick at their skin and bite their nails across all developmental periods. Further, what if the *in time* concept meant many, many years? Fortunately for my situation, Dr. P was correct and in time I would stop. Unfortunately, *BFRB*'s do not have a predetermined expiration date and the stop point is different for each person. Sometimes, left untreated, the end date can be nonexistent or irrelevant.

# 5

My parents took Dr. P's rather cautious suggestion to visit a child psychologist and found a doctor a little distance east from where we lived. My after school visits to the psychologist, became as routine as dance classes. I definitely did not want to go. What child actually likes going to the doctor? I was, however, smart enough to realize that although I did not want to visit a strange man in business attire and did not want to stop picking, I definitely wanted to keep from getting caught. Being a perfectionist, I also did not want to continue to disappoint my parents. Looking back, I was in denial. This is no surprise, however, given my age at that time.

I was still in second grade when I began my visits to the psychologist, Dr. Fred. At this point, my nail biting and skin picking were out of control. Day after day, it was getting more difficult to cover my arms and legs from my parents. They were willing to do anything to find answers and get me help, and I was willing to do anything to keep them from seeing what my body looked like. As adults and amazing parents, they were always smarter and lifetimes ahead of me. I often thought that if I wore long sleeves and pants to school, and long johns at night for pajamas, there was no way they would ever see. It was no surprise that wearing a full body covering in the middle of summer in

Florida was all they needed to see to know that I was covering my picking. This only led to my parents' desire to reveal what was being hidden. Unfortunately, the long johns were a give-away and the shame of disappointing my parents was enough punishment.

My parents never punished me for my actions. I remember the conversation they had with Dr. Fred. He made sure to tell them that this was not something that was punishable behavior or worthy of time out. This is a very important point. As with any *BFRB's*, one of the worst things a parent can do is punish their child. Fighting sometimes occurs amongst family members over what to do for these seemingly uncontrollable behaviors. Parents may scold or punish their child, as this is a standard parenting practice to change an undesired behavior.

According to B.F. Skinner's behavioral therapy or behavior modification, it seems fairly straightforward. A reinforcer is a stimulus or a thing. Positive reinforcement can be thought of as adding something to an environment or situation to increase the likelihood of a response. Negative reinforcement is just the opposite as one takes something away to increase a response in the future. Punishment is often used in parenting, in the form of scolding, yelling, or spanking. Punishment is adding something unpleasant to an environment or a situation to decrease a response in the future. Behavior modification appears to be clear-cut, yet it can still be applied incorrectly. With children who have not yet reached a level of verbal expression or emotional intelligence to participate in talk therapy, behavior therapy is most successful.

So, why is punishment incorrect for parents who are targeting *BFRB's*? The reason punishment works outside of this context is because a child learns to associate an unpleasant experience with the behavior. The way to reduce or eliminate the unpleasant experience is to reduce the behavior. In the case of *BFRB's*, the picking, pulling, or biting behavior is a symptom of something deeper: feelings of anxiety, stress, overwhelming emotions, unhappiness, and/or boredom. The child views such behaviors as being uncontrollable.

What this means is the parents are punishing their child for something that the child deems to be out of his or her control. Taking this one step further, the child may think that he or she is being punished for their lack of control, not the behavior itself. Such lack of restraint is present in children all the way through teenage years, even if there is not a BFRB of focus, as this is a normal part of development. Why do the majority of children and teenagers make many bad decisions and act before thinking? The prefrontal cortex, which is the portion of the brain protected by the forehead, is still in development.

Dr. Fred's office was on the top floor of a strip center of medical offices. I would climb countless steps to get to his office, and it felt like such a trek for my little legs. His office was rather unique as it emulated a California beach bungalow but was located in Florida. The walls were wooden, and the shaggy carpet was an ugly brown. There were skylights and wood beams across the ceiling. I found it rather odd that he had a desk with a large bookcase filled with brick-like psychology textbooks alongside a sofa. Why was there a sofa? The only doctor's office I had been to prior to my first visit with Dr. Fred was Dr. P's, who worked in a cheerful, colorful office tailored to children. Instead of looking at *Highlight* magazines for children, I was staring at stark, intimidating books collecting dust on his shelf. There was no scale or cold metal examination table in sight. I also did not see a sink for hand washing or a blood pressure cuff. What kind of doctor did he claim to be, and how did he get this past my parents who were so smart? There had to be a catch.

Keeping in mind I was in second grade, the target treatment was behavioral therapy. The other common treatment options at this age include art therapy, play therapy, or a very limited version of talk/cognitive therapy. The first session began with my parents and Dr. Fred behind closed doors while I sat in the waiting room. I sat and picked because there was nothing better to do. After almost thirty minutes, it was finally my turn. My first therapy session, just like all the rest, was not terrifying at all. I found it to be rather relaxing. I spent the majority of my sessions lying on the sofa staring at the ceiling. Sometimes I would close my eyes, but I also wanted to pay attention. Although I did not want to go to therapy, I did not have a choice and therefore wanted to make sure, just like everything else in my life, that I was the best patient he had ever had. I was, again, striving for perfection even in my therapy sessions.

My parents implemented a sticker chart at home at the request of Dr. Fred. I would earn a sticker for each day I did not bite my nails or pick. Each evening we would count how many marks I had on my body as a form of monitoring and day-to-day comparison. A certain amount of stickers resulted in a prize. I liked this idea. Dr. Fred was not so bad after all. My parents told the doctor that they recognized that the majority of my nail biting and skin picking occurred in the evening once I was in bed or right before going to bed. I never had a fear of going to sleep or the dark, so it did not appear to be fear-based behaviors. Perhaps it was just my way of winding down after a full day of school and activities.

Dr. Fred created a personalized cassette tape that I listened to nightly on my boom box or walkman headphones. I found the tape to be very relaxing as he spoke to me by name and used a lot of encouragement and positivity. Dr. Fred also asked me to keep my own chart, which would provide an honest self-monitoring of how many times each day I picked my skin or bit my nails. This did not really work because I did not want to be honest and appear to be failing as a patient. Sometimes my charts were accurate but typically I chose to leave out several times during the day when I was active. This tactic made me look a little better, like

I was improving. Aside from the self-monitoring, I was spending so much time charting, in therapy, and listening to Dr. Fred's tape that I certainly wanted to think that my behaviors were abating.

Of all the work that was done in therapy with Dr. Fred, the part that left the greatest impression was what took place in the classroom. Treating children with mental health disorders undoubtedly requires a collaborative team effort. My parents had a parent-teacher conference with my second grade teacher, Mrs. U. She was truly a remarkable teacher, known for being strict yet understanding. I learned so much from her teaching skills during my second grade school year. Mrs. U also implemented behavioral intervention with the guidance from my parents, at the request of my doctor. I was very embarrassed that my parents had told my teacher what I was doing. I also needed to keep in mind that if therapy was ever going to end, my parents needed to do what they were advised to do. Mrs. U was made aware of my nail biting and my skin picking, and she never said one word to me about it. She never pulled me aside to tell me she had a meeting with my parents. I was treated no different than before the meeting but for one exception. My parents told me that there was a system that would be started. One of the struggles of *BFRB's* is coming to the realization or conscious awareness of what I am doing at that moment in time that I am engaging in the unhealthy behavior.

I could expect that starting the following school day, when

Mrs. U was standing behind the wooden podium at the front of the class, she would do something different that only she and I knew about. I was to continue to watch my teacher and be the very attentive student that I always was. As teachers tend to continuously scan the classroom for behaviors to praise or punish, if she saw me biting my nails or touching my skin, she would simply wait for me to make eye contact with her and then raise a finger. This signal was my indication that she saw me and that I needed to stop. It was a great reminder. Mrs. U was also an amazing teacher because she persisted in implementing this system for the entire school year. I knew she was in constant communication with my parents to provide them additional feedback that they could relay to Dr. Fred. It certainly was amazing team work. Over time, I had no other choice but to become a team player. My behavior persisted until fifth or sixth grade.

One aspect of this whole situation with my *BFRB* experience that is still somewhat baffling is that from kindergarten until I stopped picking in early middle school, there was not one time that the children teased or bullied me for my extensive scabs. Generally, young children, who don't mean to be intrusive or rude, tend to say exactly what is on their mind. It is all too often I am in a public setting, such as the grocery store, when I see and hear a little child point and say (always extra loudly), "That man can't walk right" or "Look dad, that girl is fat." Given that this tends to be the common experience for a young child at one time or another, I should have been teased to the point of tears. This never happened. I had many male and female friends, and despite my time spent in sleeveless dance leotards, soccer shorts, and bathing suits, no one besides my parents ever seemed to notice. My brothers never said anything either. I cannot help but be incredibly thankful, as bullying is one of the most prevalent problems in the school system to date.

Just like I do not remember the day I began picking at my skin, I also do not have any recollection of the day I officially stopped. I do remember the length of time where my behavior was decreasing, and my parents continuously praised me. I know this was a genuinely happy moment in their lives. Like many, there was an ebb and flow to my *BFRB's*. At times I would do beautifully, and then I would regress without doing anything different. This is one of the challenges to treating *BFRB's* or anything else for that matter. It is hard to maintain consistency over an extended period of time. Fortunately, the results of my actions faded. Over the years my scars faded. Today, I do not have a single scar anywhere on my body as a result of my behavior, though it took over six years for the scars to fade. I know that by my senior year of high school I did not have any ramifications as a result of skin picking.

The nail biting, on the other hand, persisted a bit longer. I became used to having nubs for nails, but as I got older I absolutely despised what it looked like. I felt embarrassed. I was born with incredibly long fingers and beautiful hands. However, my nails were red, bloody, and irritated. My mother could relate as she has been a nail biter her whole life. There are many people that bite their nails, cuticles, or the surrounding skin. In my mind, it never seemed as damaging as the skin picking which led to scarring and potential infection. I tried applying a distasteful nail polish, created for nail biters, along with hot pepper; I always found a way around it. When I turned fifteen, I started going with my mother to the nail salon to get acrylics. This kept my natural nails from being accessible to my mouth. This certainly helped stop the behavior unless it was that time of the month where the old acrylic set was coming off in lieu of a new set. Then, I went right back to biting my nicely grown nails despite the time without nail biting.

It was not until my second year of graduate school that I just stopped. I do not know why it was at that moment in my life, but that is when it simply happened. There is really no other way to describe it other than to say that it lost appeal, and I grew bored and tired of the nail biting. I believe that there is always positive that comes from negative. To this day, there has not been one occurrence where I have taken for granted the opportunity to get a manicure with my natural nails. Every time I make the drive, it is such an exceptional gift to myself and elicits such placid and happy emotions. I never knew how beautiful my natural nails were because I never gave my nails the chance to be and look how they were intended. Now, picking out a new nail polish to add to my collection has an entirely different meaning: one of triumph, freedom, and persistence. In sum, I am grateful.

PART 2
# TRICHOTILLOMANIA

# 6

After just twenty-nine years, I learned that there are always going to be challenges. Granted, I knew this many years ago. When you overcome one hurdle, you turn to face a new one, which may or may not be of the same height, duration, and weight. I wish I could say that my challenges with working through my skin, nail, and perfectionism issues were the beginning and end to my hurdles. Even today, it almost brings me to tears to think that I went through so much as a child. At that time, most other children did not even know what a psychologist was.

Currently, psychologists and counselors are more common in and out of the school system when working with children. As our field has advanced in precise diagnosis (i.e. determining what is wrong) and treatments proven to work based on scientific research, our society has grown more accustomed to reading about Autism research or hearing about the increased prevalence, or commonness, of Attention - Deficit/Hyperactivity Disorder on the news, for example. In the 1980's and 1990's, the psychology research was less, as was research funding and education for the public on psychology topics. Therefore my parents felt somewhat isolated in finding answers, and I did not know of another classmate that did what I did at the time.

Comparing never gets us anywhere other than down, but

almost everyone does it. If I really did want to compare, I could step back and realize that there are many children who had it worse than I did. Yet, that is always going to be the case. There will always be someone better off and worse off than where I am or where you are at this moment in life. Yet, that never made me feel better. I felt that it was solely a deterrent to acknowledging how I was feeling when struggling. All I wanted was for my feelings to be actualized…regarded…accepted.

We all do it or have done it at some point. We compare ourselves to celebrities, family, friends, spouses, teammates, coworkers, classmates, and even people we don't know but see in day-to-day life. In actuality, comparing yourself yesterday to yourself today is the best way to get ahead and reach your true potential. It did not take me many years to learn this, but it took many years to actually initiate and practice this concept. If you really feel the need to compete with someone, compete with yourself. Each day is a new opportunity to learn something, experience something, or share something, so use the sunrise as an opportunity to be better than you were at yesterday's sunset.

On that note, I am the first person to admit that it is easier said than done. My life was no *Pollyanna* and having a competitive nature was fuel to the Trichotillomania fire. The last thing I ever wanted to do was to compare my hair and my looks to my friends who had their natural hair. To reiterate, withholding comparison was easier said than done and when I did, I felt sorry for myself and questioned why I was the chosen one to be tortured by my own actions.

# 7

By sixth grade, I was able to close the door to skin picking and nail biting. I turned right around only to run face first into a steel door; a door that was child's play to open and overwhelmingly brutal to close. Over the years, my parents have questioned me.

"So, why did you start? When did you start? Where did you get the idea to pull your hair?"

These questions are neither unusual nor uncommon among parents of children or teenagers with Trichotillomania. The name, Trichotillomania, sounds gargantuan and intimidating. In my experience, those words precisely captured my struggle.

My middle school and high school education were spent at the same private Christian school where I attended with the same faces for all seven years. The faculty and staff were very involved in the students' lives during school hours as well as what we did on the weekends. It was during my seventh grade year that everything changed. To clarify what I mean by *everything*, I mean my life, as a whole, forever.

Due to my attendance at a Christian school, daily religion class was mandatory just like all other core subjects. Additionally, we were required to take physical education the first half of the year and health the latter part of the year. One day in my all-girls health class, my health instructor, who also happened to be the religion instructor, told the class that we would be doing an exercise to work on self-confidence and group cohesiveness. It was also a great way to mitigate the competition among girls, which is exceptional during middle school. We had never done anything like this.

Our desks were aligned in rows and my teacher, Miss Bee, stood at the front of the room to explain the exercise.

"For the rest of the period, we are going to take time to pay a compliment to each classmate. This will provide each of you an opportunity to not only recognize a positive attribute in each person in the room, but at the end of the exercise you will have a complete list of compliments given by each of your peers. What you will leave this class period with is a reminder of how much you are loved and appreciated."

We each received one sheet of paper. Written at the top was a name of one of the girls in my health class. The page was sectioned off into sixteen spaces to represent the sixteen girls sitting in class that day. I was handed a piece of paper from my teacher, and the name *Nicole* was written at the top. This meant I had to write a compliment to Nicole in the first space. I then covered my one-lined appreciation and passed Nicole's page to Jessie who was sitting right behind me. It was Jessie's turn to write something special to Nicole in space two. She was not able to see my written accolade so as not to copy it. Every girl in the class went about this process with a rotation to the next classmate's page occurring approximately every thirty seconds.

At the end of health period, my teacher handed me a page with *Lindsey* written at the top followed by sixteen hand written compliments. Some sentiments were written in standard ballpoint pen, some in glittery gel pens, and some in pencil. Of the sixteen compliments, seven read either, "You have the most beautiful hair in the grade," or, "I love your hair and wish mine looked like it." My parents called me *Hair Bear* for a reason.

I had long, thick, light brown hair with caramel and honey colored highlights. My hair glistened in the sun and always required multiple hair ties to secure it in a ponytail during sports practice. My hair was one of the few things I was known for among the girls in the middle school. I cannot help but think of what an enigma I was handed in life. I have been told that the things you most take for granted are the things that will be the first to be taken right from under you.

Whoever came to this realization, long before I lived it, is ingenious.

My seventh grade homeroom class consisted of approximately twenty students and a pregnant homeroom teacher, who also taught English to the entire grade. When I initially think of the formidable middle school years, I think of awkwardness, lankiness, social ineptitude, and the unrestrained hormone *pandemic*. My experience was different. Aside from the volatile mood swings and striving to become even more perfectionistic in academia and appearance, my social life was thriving, and I was one of the most popular students among teachers and peers. I was a good friend, a respectful daughter, and a hard worker. I cared for others, and went out of my way to make sure each person in my grade felt important.

Part way into the seventh grade year, my homeroom teacher, having a difficult pregnancy, was replaced by a substitute. My teacher's doctor ordered her to stay confined to bed for the duration of her pregnancy. The substitute teacher was a nice older lady who looked like a librarian. She wore thick eyeglasses with a pearl chain that allowed her glasses to hang like a necklace when not in use. It took some time for everyone to get accustomed to a new face at 8:10 am each morning. The substitute had her way of running the homeroom class and English class. Not only was her teaching style unique, but also, the day the new teacher came into class, so did a new student.

The new female student sat meekly in the back corner of the classroom right near the teacher's desk. On the first day, she seemed overly nervous, beyond that of a new student on his or her first day. My substitute teacher introduced herself and alerted the class that she would be our teacher for the remainder of the school year. She then introduced the new student.

"I am sure at this point all of you have recognized the one additional body in this classroom. I would like to introduce you to my daughter, Emily. Emily has been homeschooled her whole life, but she is also in seventh grade. Now that I am taking the time to be your teacher, Emily will have to learn in the classroom instead of at home."

While this certainly was unexpected, it was not anything that the class had difficulty in accepting.

Before the end of my seventh grade year, we made one field trip hosted by the English department to see a Shakespearean play performed at a local performing arts center. A notice went home to parents asking for volunteer drivers. On the day of the field trip, we did not have rotating classes as usual. Instead, we spent the morning taking attendance, listening to morning announcements on the loudspeaker, and then discussing the field trip. Instead of the students choosing what mom and friends they wanted to ride with, my teacher separated the class. Unfortunately, I was drafted to the substitute teacher's car accompanied by her daughter, Emily, and one other female student who evenly matched Emily's unassuming presence. I rode in the passenger's seat.

While on our way to the performance, I could not help but think about the fun my friends were having in the other cars. I knew I was missing out on talking, laughing, and radio entertainment. My car consisted of crickets chirping. The only break to the silence was when Emily, in the seat directly to the rear of her mother, excitedly uttered,

"Mom, I see one. You have a grey hair at the back of

your head."

"Where, where? Get it!" Emily reached forward and plucked the single gray strand from her mother's jet black, kinky haired scalp.

In that moment I felt uncomfortable as if there was an invasion of privacy (although I am not sure whose privacy). I had never before seen an interaction like this and also was unaware that women mysteriously pulled gray hairs from their scalp. Given that I had been coloring and highlighting my hair for a few years, my mind had never even questioned my hair's various colors. Something about being a witness to this mother-daughter exchange caused so much strong emotion that I continued to replay it over and over in my mind. I felt awkward, uncomfortable, confused and embarrassed. Perhaps my teacher also thought it was an awkward moment for such a behavior because she offered further information.

"Sorry about that. I am too cheap to get my hair colored at the salon, and I don't like how it looks when I color my own hair." She laughed. "Emily has become really good at helping me search for the bad, gray hairs."

We arrived to the performing arts center, and I reunited with my friends to watch the play as intended. It may be somewhat preposterous to say that the day I drove in the car with my substitute teacher was the precipitating event to set off a cataclysmic chain of reactions, but it was. That was all it took.

That was my so-called traumatic event that my parents often wondered about. I have no further explanation as to how the steel door, marked *Trichotillomania*, opened.

# 8

The hair pulling behavior officially entered my life the first time I washed my hair after the field trip/car ride awkwardness. At the time I did not know what I was starting, for it would be a catastrophic decade-long snowball effect. I had been blow drying and flat ironing my hair since the beginning of seventh grade, which now seems awfully coincidental given that this was also when I began pulling my hair. I had established a hair care regimen, which ultimately led to hairstyle perfection in my opinion.

After the usual lather-rinse-condition-rinse process, I then began to dry my golden brown hair, which at the time had honey colored highlights. Due to the steam fogging my bathroom mirror combined with the heat exposure, I plugged my blow dryer and flat iron into the electrical socket in my bedroom behind my full-length white wicker mirror. With my black barrel hairbrush in one hand and blow dryer in the other, I began to dry my hair section by section. This was the only way to dry my hair since I had so much of it. When the back and sides were dry, straight and acceptable, I took the center crown portion and dried it by pulling the whole section straight up toward my ceiling. I did this over and over until it was dry. The *straight up* technique always helped me to achieve a voluminous look. Once complete,

I took the front hairline section and brushed it straight down in front of my face. My dampened hair hung in front of my eyes, nose, and mouth like a curtain. Next, I used my flat black paddle brush with black bristles to grab the hair and pull it straight down while I used my free hand to follow along with the nozzle of the blow dryer. The *straight down* technique allowed my hair to part nicely down the middle and frame my face.

On this particular night, when working on the *straight down* portion, I, due to the car ride a few days prior, paid extra close attention to two things; one, to the contrast between my hair color and the black brush bristles, and two, to the variations of color in my own hair due to the professional color job and highlights (of which many shades of blonde were used). Repetitively, I continued to watch my hair run through the brush bristles and with each full brush-through, my hair colors became more noticeable as my hair dried.

With my hair now completely dry and hanging in my face, combined with the illuminating light from my ceiling fan, I was able to see more clearly the highlighted pieces. I sandwiched my hair in between my index and middle finger, so it was taut like strings on a violin, with each individual strand parallel to the next. Within the approximately fifteen to twenty strands I held in my view, I scanned and compared to find the lightest one in the bunch. Essentially, I was looking to pick out the one that looked the most unlike the others. I found the first hair and carefully isolated it from the rest. I then followed that single strand up until I made it to where the tips of my thumb and index finger met my hairline, right in the front of my head. At the same time, I pulled back my thumb and index finger and removed my first strand of hair.

As for many individuals with Trichotillomania, the pulling process did not end there. I was not yet finished with that single strand of hair. Who would have ever thought that individual strands of hair held such value? The root, for several reasons, fascinated me. Given that my natural hair color is dark brown, and I had removed a colored piece, I found delight in how the strand looked running through my fingers as the dark brown gradually faded to near platinum. It reminded me of what it was like to look through a kaleidoscope of changing colors. Aside from the color, the types of roots also captivated me. Some are black, wet, shiny bulbs that stick to anything they come in contact with. Some roots are dull and white. And some are actual loops.

After the first strand, I repeated the same steps with an additional fifteen to twenty sections of hair in the same front area. Again. And again. And again. Without reason, I eventually stopped and went on with my night, which involved studying in bed and talking on the house phone with two friends via a three-way phone call. My first night of pulling had nothing to do with what I physically felt, as the hair was pulled from my head, and it had nothing to do with my emotional state. The point of the activity, which lasted fifteen minutes at most, was to isolate and remove the discordant pieces, and create my own rendition of the witnessed hair pull from days prior.

My pulling act did not qualify me as having a mental health disorder. Technically, I did not yet meet the diagnosis of Trichotillomania. In psychology, clinicians use a hefty textbook, known as the *Diagnostic and Statistical Manual of Mental Disorders, 5th Edition (DSM-5),* with page after page of criteria in order to determine a diagnosis for a given individual. I view it as the *know all* book of psychology. It is the text psychologists turn to for answers and clarification when it comes time for diagnosing the problem. At times, this is a slippery slope as it may be difficult for beginning clinicians to determine order from disorder, or normal behavior from abnormal behavior. We are all human, and none of us are perfect. Therefore, we all have quirks and oddities, some of which mimic parts of disorders. If you were to pick up a copy of the *DSM-5,* turn to the *Personality Disorders* section, select a Personality Disorder, and read the list of criteria, you might feel compelled to self-diagnose. We all have a little of this and a little of that. Some of us have more than others. Yet, none of it qualifies as a true diagnosed disorder. You see, just because one criterion is present in your own life does not mean that it is a problem or negatively impacting quality of life. I had pulled a few strands of my own hair, yet it was neither problematic nor impairing. Do not be alarmed in reflecting upon

47

your own life if you happen to skim through the *DSM-5*.

Two nights passed before I washed my hair again. And two nights passed before I pulled a few more strands from the front hairline section in the same manner I had done the first time. Apparently, I was looking for the next lightest hairs that hung among my mane. Looking back at the start of my disorder, I cannot help but feel empathic for my hair. What did it ever do to me to deserve such cruel treatment?

The same thing went on the next time I washed and dried my hair. My wash-dry-pull cycle, much like the wash-dry-wear of your clothes and laundry room activities, became routine. At this preliminary stage, I had neither specific identifiable thoughts nor emotions toward the process. I doubt anyone has alarming thoughts or emotions toward washing and drying their clothes. (Okay, perhaps there is some feet dragging, delay, procrastination involved when it is time to do laundry.) My experience was much the same. It was an effortful, lengthy process to wash my hair. At times I would put it off until I broke a really good sweat during my extracurricular activities. I became so accustomed to the process that I never looked in the mirror when I was done drying my hair. I knew it looked right without seeing it. Then, I would continue with wrapping up the rest of the night before bed.

But, there was one morning unlike any other. My alarm went off at 6:15 am, and I grudgingly emerged from my warm, fluffy bed. I was not, and may never be, a morning person. Due to my attendance at private school, my predetermined apparel was always laid out the night before. I had several options to choose from: a school-emblem collared shirt with khaki pants, a school-emblem collared shirt with navy pants, a school-emblem collared shirt with navy shorts (at or below my knees), a school-emblem collared shirt with a plaid skirt (touching my knees or to the ankle), or a button-down Oxford school-emblem shirt with any of the aforementioned bottoms. This particular morning I put on my khaki pants with a navy blue collared shirt accompanied by a required belt and my navy blue and white Sketcher shoes. Then, I went into the bathroom.

I began to brush my teeth in the dark. I needed some time for my eyes to take to the light, and I had not yet put in my contacts, so I could not see anyway. After the pearly whites were sparkling, I washed and dried my face, then reached for my contact case. I am near blind without my contacts yet always manage to find my clothes and toothbrush in the morning. I flipped the light switch on over my vanity and carefully gave myself vision. I could see my reflection staring back at me. "Wait a second," I thought to myself. "There must be something wrong with these contacts. Perhaps I mixed up the prescription between my eyes?" I blinked a few times in an attempt to correct my eyesight. Blinking only made what I thought I had seen even more frightful. I moved my face closer to the mirror to take a closer look and my world went dark and blurred. I could barely stand to look at myself any longer, so I sat on the toilet seat cover and my eyes filled with tears. I felt a mix of emotions, which included fear, panic, sadness, anger, confusion, and stress. I remember the feelings well.

I had exactly ten minutes to apply my makeup and cover my blotchy face, eliminate the redness and puffiness from around my eyes, and act tickled pink. Even without my morning nourishment, my mental processing speed kicked in at this moment. I grabbed a cloth headband, which I almost never wore to school. I put it on to conceal a specific area, finished up my morning routine, and was downstairs in time to meet my brothers and mother for the ride to school. They knew and saw nothing out of the ordinary.

# 9

The truth was blown wide open that evening. After a rather mundane school day, I came home to complete my academic duties and followed it with a quick shower. I was hoping that the reflection I saw in the mirror that morning was more observable to my eyes than anyone else's. If I wore a headband downstairs for dinner it absolutely would have been questioned, as I never wore a headband after a shower. I had a momentary recollection of my mother and father asking to see my arms and legs when I entered the room with long johns in the summer. My parents always knew. I discarded the headband idea and decided to go with just a t-shirt and pajama pants, as usual.

Dinner with the family was a requirement. Unless there was a pertinent obligation (such as a practice or game) which prevented one of us from being home for family dinner, the five of us always ate as a family. Sometimes my mother would cook, as she is a great cook, or sometimes we would order food for delivery. Regardless, every night we all sat around our large oak dining table to eat and reflect on the day's highs and lows. Due to the size of the table, the five of us would gather at one end with my father at the head, my mother and I on one side, and my two brothers on the opposing side. An oblong three-bulb chandelier of sorts illuminated our dining room table. The light fixture hovered over the table approximately three feet from the tabletop to provide adequate lighting.

Typically, I helped to prepare the meal or set the table. On this night, due to my colossal workload, I descended from my room when I heard dinner was served. When I walked into the dining room area, my father was sitting and focused on the plates to which he was serving portions of pasta. My mother had her back to me as she was spooning meatballs and sauce from a large pot. My brothers were in the middle of some verbal exchange. I sat in my usual spot just as my mother sat and my brother proceeded to say a prayer:

"Thank you, God, for this day and for everything you have given us. Please bless this meal and continue to watch over us, guide us, and protect us. Amen."

It was no more than two minutes and four bites into my meal when it happened.

"Oh my god! Lindsey, look at me! LOOK AT ME!" I knew where we were headed.

"What? What is wrong?"

I replied as if nothing was wrong while attempting to keep my head straightforward but glanced at my mom from the corner of my eye. My brothers both looked up.

"Mom, what is wrong? What's happening?"

At this point, my face was crimson. I could not stop it from happening. This is the natural tendency when I am caught in a lie, doing something wrong, or put on the spot. As one who strives for perfection, this does not happen often, but when it does, I want to hide.

"Lindsey, turn your head right now. Look at me." I listened to her.

"Lindsey, what happened to your hairline? OH MY GOD! The entire front section of your hair is missing. What happened?"

The sound in my mother's voice and the look on my father's face was that of fear, panic, and concern to say the least. Honestly, their reactions likely would not have been all too different if I would have lifted up my shirt and exposed a baby bump at age fourteen.

I was completely silent. My mind was flooded with emotion, which prevented the formation of logical, cohesive thoughts. My father, always the calmer of the two, collectedly said, "Lindsey, just tell us what happened. We will understand."

My mouth was paralyzed, and my lips were sealed. I did not know what I should say. I could feel my mouth growing dry. Do I tell the truth or do I lie? If I lie, what would be the most believable fib? I took a moment for serenity and clarity. The silence enabled my mother to start offering various possibilities of what she thought happened.

"Did you try to cut your hair? Did you shave your face and forehead? Were you using a razor to try to even your hairline?"

Any of those options sounded good. I toiled with the notion

53

of agreeing. I looked from my father to my mother and back to my father. I now had everyone's attention. I swallowed hard.

"I...I....I....pulled it out. It was an accident. I am sorry."

That was it. I lost it. I reached my breaking point. I could not say another word. The tears overwhelmed me, and I began to hyperventilate. I ran from the table and sprinted up the wooden staircase nearly in flight. For the next hour, I found my home in the back corner of my closet. I did not want to be found. I curled up in the fetal position, let the clothes hang in front of me, and cried. There was nothing else I could do.

An hour passed, and I saw no one. I was exhausted, had a pounding headache, and was depleted of tears. I knew that my family was downstairs, most likely not eating, but trying to decide what to say, what to do, and what to think. I had provided them with a rather odd truth. It was something that neither of them would have ever guessed which was not surprising. I came out of my closet and cracked my bedroom door just enough to hear what was going on downstairs. I heard silverware clinking with dishes, which meant the family, was clearing the dinner from the table. There was no conversation. I closed the door and went back into hiding. Shortly thereafter, there was a knock on my bedroom door.

"Linds?" It was my father. "Linds? Where are you? I want to talk to you."

I felt extreme guilt for hurting my parents, as my father

sounded distraught. I emerged from my closet holding my hand over my hairline, much like what someone would do when they had a headache. At that moment, I felt as if I would never want to remove my palm from my forehead, ever.

"Dad, I am really sorry. I don't even know what to say or do. I totally ruined everything, and I am so embarrassed." For now, I was able to speak. My father was sitting on my bed.

"Lindsey, we are sorry this happened, but we are going to do whatever it takes to get you help. Your mother has been downstairs on the computer researching. We learned that there is a name for this and that there are tons of other people who do the same thing."

I was beside myself.

"What? A name? What do you mean? How can that be? I did not learn this from anyone or see it anywhere. What do you mean? This is a real thing?"

I was honestly shocked yet felt a sense of relief. At the same time, I was not at all convinced that I had a *thing* going on. This was a one-time situation. Well, to clarify, this was a one-week situation.

"Linds, please come downstairs with me. Your mom has found some great information, and we want to talk to you together. Whatever is going on, we are going to help you." My father embraced me, and I knew it would be all right.

Together we went downstairs. My dinner plate was still sitting on the dining room table in isolation. I, too, felt isolated. My father took my hand and led me into the computer room where my mom was focused on the computer screen. She stood up and did not say a word. She enclosed me in her arms and kissed my forehead.

"Lindsey, it is going to be okay."

At this moment I felt comforted by having such caring, nurturing, understanding parents. I felt guilt for upsetting them. I felt fear for the recognition of what I had done. I felt stress for the fleeting thoughts that kept surfacing of what the future would hold with a nonexistent, screwy hairline. My father pulled up two chairs to the computer desk and the three of us, together, huddled around the screen. The light hurt my eyes, and my headache persisted. I had a hard time reading the computer screen, for at this moment I was emotionally drained, mentally overloaded, and nutritionally famished. My brothers came into the room, hugged me, and told me they loved me and were sorry. My parents and I buckled down for the next hour to begin our education on a unique mental health disorder with a rather intimidating name. It was this very evening in 1998 that Trichotillomania formally introduced itself.

# 10

The night we sat down to research, we learned the following. The diagnosable mental disorder of Trichotillomania is defined as the irresistible recurrent pulling of one's own hair resulting in noticeable hair loss, and causing significant impairment and distress. In adult Trichotillomania, there are more reported cases in females than males, among Caucasians. For the majority diagnosed, hair pulling occurs in multiple contexts: when alone, in the presence of others, in the car, at the computer, or at work, for example. Hair may be pulled from any site on the body from which hair grows. The most common body sites are eyebrows, eyelashes, and scalp, yet some individuals pull from arms, legs, or the pubic region.

Mature Trichotillomania has a high rate of occurrence with many psychiatric conditions including Mood Disorders, Attention-Deficit/Hyperactivity Disorder, Anxiety Disorders, Substance Abuse, and Personality Disorders. Although it may appear as though the disorder is not very common in the general population due to hesitancy to seek treatment out of embarrassment and shame, the estimated prevalence rate is three to five percent across the developmental lifespan. The occurrence in older adolescents and young adults is estimated to range between one and four percent. While the exact widespread presence of Trichotillomania among young children and infants is currently unknown, it is estimated to be more widespread then amongst mature individuals and more balanced across boys and girls. Further, the disorder has been around for years, but there has been a growing awareness among parents, psychologists, and researchers, especially within the last fifteen to twenty years, of how this disorder may impair everyday living by causing distress, academic, occupational, and financial difficulties, physical discomfort, and psychosocial and interpersonal challenges.

While clinicians and practitioners are learning more on a daily basis, there is still more research to glean. As a result, it is rare that two clinicians who are not specialized in the disorder would agree on a treatment approach. Some view hair pulling as a habit and would be most likely to apply behavior therapy. This is what was used to treat my skin picking as a child. Some view hair pulling, like skin picking, as a pure behavior, without much focus on emotion and thought influences. Other clinicians may see the disorder as falling somewhere along the spectrum of Anxiety Disorders, like Obsessive Compulsive Disorder, and thereby create a treatment plan around the reduction of anxiety. The most common treatment for Trichotillomania is medication, despite the fact that hair pulling is largely unresponsive to any type of medication.

In the *DSM-5*, which provides criteria in order to make the proper diagnosis, the following Trichotillomania criteria is noted:

A) Recurrent pulling out of one's hair, resulting in hair loss;

B) Repeated attempts to decrease or stop the hair-pulling behavior;

C) The hair pulling causes clinically significant distress or impairment in social, occupational, or other important areas of functioning;

D) The hair pulling or hair loss cannot be attributed to another medical condition (e.g., a dermatologic condition); and

E) The hair pulling cannot be better explained by the symptoms of another mental disorder (eg, attempts to improve a perceived defect or flaw in appearance, such as may be observed in body dysmorphic disorder).

In addition to understanding the definitive aspects of the disorder as outlined in the *DSM-5*, two functions of hair pulling have been identified: automatic and focused. It has been stated that the automatic type is habit-like and unconscious in nature. For those who are mild to moderate nail biters, this is similar to the experience of being at work and reading an email while biting your nails. You are doing it, but you do not acknowledge that you are. The focused type occurs in more conscious awareness as a response to emotion. Although the individual may not recognize the current emotional state, he or she recognizes the current behavior.

Given the number of years I have spent learning about, researching, and experiencing the disorder firsthand, I developed my own ideas as to what drives the hair pulling behavior and other *BFRB*'s. All humans strive for internal homeostasis on many levels. Homeostasis, in this case, is being in a comfortable state. The main function of the hypothalamus (control center of the brain) is homeostasis, or maintaining the body's *status quo*. Factors such as blood pressure, body temperature, fluid and electrolyte balance, and body weight are held to a precise value called the *set point*. Although this set point can migrate over time, day to day it is remarkably fixed. My belief is that the automatic-type hair pulling functions as an internal regulator of attention in the highs and lows of daily activity. The automatic type may be more closely related to the emotional regulation function of focused pulling than previously thought. Like other factors of an individual that need to be regulated, I believe that each individual has an attention comfort level and an attention threshold (attention in terms of mental attentiveness), hence the reason why some can sit and focus for longer periods of time than others. Attentional capacity, also known as sustained attention, also depends on the present task and how interesting or captivating it may be for that individual.

My belief is that when an individual is given tasks that demand their attention at a comfortable level, he or she will engage in the task without hair pulling. However when there is a task or responsibility given to a person during their day which require too little or too much work (i.e. the task becomes overly difficult, long-lasting, and attention demands escalate, or the task is under-captivating, uninteresting, or too easy, and attention demands drop significantly), this is when the individual engages in the hair pulling. My hair pulling always occurred when I was in a state of low attentional demand, such as riding in the car, watching television, on the phone, at my computer desk, or laying in bed. These situations are times when there is under activation of my brain functioning similar to that of boredom. I also pulled my hair during opposite situations, brain overload, such as multi-tasking, studying difficult material, or persisting in mental tasks despite being fatigued and wanting to shut down. From the patients I have seen in practice, it is rare that patients report hair pulling while engaged in physical activity (running, walking, skipping), or eating. These are tasks, which likely falls into an individual's *comfort level* as it relates to demand of attention, and hair pulling does not occur.

It is important to recognize that my perspective is one individual's viewpoint on a complex disorder. This is where research becomes important to test whether one perspective, or hypothesis, is right or wrong. Nonetheless, it may be of benefit to consider such ideas, or this may even ring true with those readers who have experience with hair pulling.

# 11

My hair pulling behavior went from the size of an ant mound to a Swiss Alps monstrosity in no time. What began as an idea and a concept to remove the lightest hairs turned into a full-blown disorder. By the end of my seventh grade year, I had a two-inch hairline recession, which almost ran the span of my forehead. Unlike the *classic taper* or *classic fade*, popular men's hair styles of the 90's and 2000's, my hairline was uneven in addition to the various black hair roots that were popping through my scalp at different times. Further, I would have never opted for this look, as it put a huge hindrance on my strivings for a perfect appearance. I do not recall exactly how things progressed with the rate of my pulling behavior, but I know it happened quickly.

Due to the time that had passed since pulling from my hairline combined with self-analysis, I gradually recognized that I did not enjoy the pulling behavior itself. Instead, I was after the sensation at the root when the hair was removed. The most relatable example is the experience of being bitten by a red ant. Typically, one does not enjoy the act of moving his nails over the region of the bite. An *arm and hand motion* is done for the physical sensation of relief or pleasure when the itch is reduced. It is very similar to hair pulling. To those who have not experienced hair pulling, it seems like it is a painful act, yet there is nothing painful about it when done successfully one strand at a time.

While pulling strand after strand often exhausted my hand, fingers, and arm, I found that I persisted to reap the benefit of that second of euphoric greatness. Because the feeling really lasts for such a miniscule amount of time, it left me always going back for more. I would also bypass the fatigue by switching hands. Additionally, I recognized that I enjoyed the surprise of what was going to be at the end of the hair, which is all too reminiscent of my wonderment when I was young and squeezed my pick marks. What was going to be extracted, and what would it look like?

Roots come in all shapes, sizes and colors, and that fascinated me. I felt very scientific and exploratory when I was looking at the end. After looking at the end, I had a few different things I would do with the hair. In no particular order or any identifiable purpose, I would either drop the hair allowing it to land as it may, stick the root to my white notebook paper (I was amazed how roots were wet and sticky but then became dry), or I would bite off the very end of the root and toss the rest of the hair away. Eating the root was neither done as a late night snack nor as a way to satisfy my taste buds. Without recognizing at the time, I did it to further stimulate the sense of feel in my mouth.

I love sushi, but I do not like the topping delicacies. One time I ordered a particular roll, which came, topped with masago, although I had ordered the roll plain. Masago is the vibrant orange eggs, which come from a small fish. Each egg is firm, tiny, and pop-able. So as not to wave the waitress down and wait to have my sushi roll remade, I decided to scrape the eggs off the roll to the best of my ability. Due to the rather small, seed-like size of the eggs, many of them were unable to be removed. I remember picking up my first piece of sushi between my chopsticks that night and moving the roll into my mouth. As I chewed, I felt little pops between the tips of my teeth. That exact sensation, if you have ever eaten masago on a roll, is very close in experience to what it is like to pop a root off a hair between the front teeth. The action is small and momentary, but something about it is a little desirous, at least for me. For those of you who are sushi connoisseurs, I hope I have not ruined your love by drawing this parallel.

As much as I presently try to withhold self-judgment, it is hard not to scrutinize. After all, I had expectations set for greatness, and I was my own biggest critic. My current thoughts may be very similar to yours. Upon reflection, my hair pulling seems bizarre, gross, painful, twisted, and confusing.

The initial post-blow dry pulling turned into nightly pulling. I was lying in bed to study my handwritten notes for an upcoming English test. I was relaxed yet likely feeling anxious for the exam, given my teacher was tough on the class and expected a lot. I was good at English but not great. I earned grades of A or A–. I held my paper in my right hand while my left hand had somehow developed its own mind and traveled to my scalp. While touching the lower left region of my hairline about an inch in from my ear, I stumbled upon a sensitive spot that sent another strong electrical current through my body. I pulled one hair, this time ignoring the color or the root. I was focused on studying for English class while also experiencing the physical sensation of the pull. It felt much more sensitive than the front hairline. I had found my way to the next area of hair that was soon to be not much of an area of hair at all. As I studied for the next hour, my mind went to work on the words on the page of notebook paper. My left hand entered into a playground of hair-like fun. What an ironic hour to be able to master the novel *To Kill A Mockingbird* while absolutely sabotaging the lower back portion of my hairline. At least I knew how to multitask effectively!

"What had I done?" I thought to myself. Strands of dark brown hair were covering my light yellow sheets like a layer of mesh. My beautiful hair was all over my fitted sheet, flat sheet, pillowcase, t-shirt, arms, and white wicker headboard. I got out of bed to brush everything onto my light yellow carpet, which made it look dirty. I felt numb due to the shock of my visualization. Light yellow carpet covered over with brown hair is a stomach churning sight. So much damage was done in such a short time. I reached up to allow my fingertips to feel the area from which I pulled. It actually felt different than when I had started. I could feel my cold, raw scalp against my fingertips. In my mind, I anticipated what it looked like if I were to get a look in the mirror. I suddenly had a strong sensation of panic and nausea that, like a beach wave, was utterly saturating. I wanted to cry. I wanted to vomit. I wanted to press pause, rewind, and start over again. None of that happened. I just turned off my light and went to bed hoping that was the end of it. Perhaps, my disgust was enough punishment to keep me from doing it again.

My alarm went off at 6:15 am, the day began with my legs swinging down from my bed, and landing feet first onto a mat of hair. "Oh my! This is disgusting. I wish I could vacuum and make this go away." It was an unsettling feeling to have long strands of hair between my toes. If you take a moment to picture walking through the barbershop or hair salon with bare feet, you will somewhat understand my thoughts and feelings during this experience.

The next thing that came to mind, before I was able to put my school uniform on or use the bathroom, was that sometimes my mother likes to come in to clean while I am at school. I frantically squatted down next to my bed and rubbed my hands, palms down, over my yellow carpet in an attempt to gather the hair into a pile and flush it down the toilet. I was also concerned that it would clog the pipes. I was willing to take the chance.

The pile of hair looked like the hair I remove from my brush when I clean it out every two weeks, and this was from just one hour of pulling. The whole situation was overwhelming. I was damaging my body, tainting my image, causing undue stress, and creating unnecessary work. The behavior was going to be hard to uphold for two reasons. One, it was a lot of mental exertion to find a way to keep from getting caught and to remember to always clean up after myself. Two, I was also going to have to make a conscious effort, by spending extra time in the morning, to cover my hairline in the front and now the back, too. That would also require my alarm to go off at 6:00 am instead of 6:15 am. For someone who is not a morning person, this was more incentive to stop. I thought to myself, "Yes, there is no way I am doing any more of this. I am done. This is ridiculous." I got dressed as usual and put on a navy blue headband to match my uniform selection for the day. Luckily, I looked good with my hair pulled back off of my face. I went downstairs where I met my brothers and mother, who greeted me with a kiss, extra large hug, and a homemade lunch.

The school day proceeded as usual. I rocked my English exam. After school, I went straight onto the soccer field for practice. I was good at soccer, but not good enough to start. I figured I would stick it out at least one more year for the chance of getting selected for the Varsity team while in eighth grade. When my mother picked me up after school, she greeted me with a smile and a kiss. This was not unusual. However, I was surprised that she was so loving and happy given what had happened the night before. My mother had spent the day at home researching. She was so excited to tell me she found many more resources that looked noteworthy and hopeful. I knew my parents were on my side, but I still wondered to which side I belonged. Did I want me to succeed?

My parents had a lot to discuss that night over dinner. My parents had found several therapists who treated Obsessive Compulsive Disorder. At that time, in 1999, Trichotillomania was thought to be a type of Obsessive Compulsive Disorder, just like hand washing. There was a treatment center in Fort Lauderdale, Florida that was recognized as an outstanding treatment provider of Obsessive Compulsive Disorder. My parents also put a call into one of the leading experts of Trichotillomania research who had discovered the benefits of Inositol, a B-vitamin, in hair pulling cessation. My parents came across an expert, Dr. Pen, who discovered the benefits of Inositol by way of an article written in 1996. The gist of Dr. Pen's article, which summarized the original 1996 article, is as follows:

> "It seems that Inositol is converted by the body to a substance that regulates the action of serotonin within brain cells. Serotonin, as we know, is a brain transmitter chemical that has been implicated in [Obsessive Compulsive Disorder] and [Trichotillomania]. Not all of these studies were conducted in the most scientific manner, but nevertheless, my curiosity had been piqued...Further study is clearly needed. It may have implications for the future treatment of [Trichotillomania]."

I was excited and felt hopeful at the thought of being able

to take a vitamin and stop what I considered to be foolishness. Although the clinical trials supporting the benefits of Inositol were not done in controlled lab settings, or in the most scientific manner, the results were positive. My parents wanted to find out where Inositol could be purchased, which brand was of the highest quality, and what dosages were appropriate for my age and weight. We waited to hear back from Dr. Pen. They had also contacted our insurance company to gain information on treatment providers in our area that treated *BFRB*'s and accepted our insurance plan. An appointment was scheduled for the following week with a therapist, Nancy, in Fort Lauderdale, for talk therapy. Lastly, I had an appointment with a psychiatrist who also worked with Nancy at the Obsessive Compulsive Disorder Center. A therapist, a vitamin treatment, a psychiatrist, and support from my parents should fix everything. We were coming out with swinging fists and guns blazing, and this disorder was going to see its last day real soon. Before I went to bed that night my mother had two questions.

"Lindsey, before you go upstairs, please, please just tell us... why did you begin and where did the idea to pull out your hair come from?"

PART 3
# TREATMENT

# 12

I sat in class and droplets of sweat dripped from my armpits under my uniform shirt. Although I had been to a psychologist as a child, I was beyond nervous as the clock approached the time in which my mother would arrive to pick me up from school. Having a mental health disorder was so different than I had remembered it being as a child. Now, I would have to take responsibility and admit to what I had done, which was terrifying in itself. "Yes, I pull out my hair, and I like it".

The intercom came on, and I was asked to come to the front office, so I packed my things and met my mother. When I got in the car, she greeted me with a gift, which was in a small plastic bag from the local vitamin store.

"I heard back from Dr. Pen. He was kind enough to spend a considerable amount of time with me on the phone from all the way in New York." I listened attentively.

"I explained that we were new to all of this as it had just happened within the last few days. I asked for his suggestions on where to turn or what direction to take. We also discussed Inositol. I just went by the vitamin store before coming to school and luckily found it. It is a fine white powder that you mix to create a drink."

I appreciated the dedication of my mother. I took the bottle out of the bag. In my hand was a standard sized plastic bottle, which looked like most other vitamin bottles. My mother had written down the correct dosage for my body size, which was left at home with plans to begin that night. This was part one of my treatment.

After a thirty-minute car ride, we arrived to a large office building literally called the *Obsessive Compulsive Disorder Center*. I was feeling overly rattled despite having plenty of time to relax in the car. Vague memories of my childhood visits to Dr. Fred greeted me. I told myself that I had nothing to be nervous or fearful of since I had plenty of experience with this type of doctor. Besides, there would be neither blood drawn nor injections, which were two of my intolerances. As we went into the elevator, my mother told me that we would be meeting with a psychiatrist to discuss medication options, and a therapist who works with teenagers that struggle with Trichotillomania.

The waiting room was filled with nothing but Obsessive Compulsive Disorder information in the forms of manuals, workbooks, leaflets, posters, and books. There was so much information at my disposal while waiting for my appointment that I later entered into the psychiatrist's office feeling as though I could sufficiently play doctor. Before I had the opportunity to meet the psychiatrist, I was required to fill out many pages of paperwork. Half of the pages were generic medical intake forms, no different than any other doctor's office. The latter of the documents were rating scales, charts, graphs, and assessment inventories. I was required to disclose a surplus of information as it pertained to my personality, my relationship with family and friends, and questions specific to behaviors. A lot of the forms, I thought, were asking questions that were general or irrelevant to my life:

*How often do you count in your head?* I do not count.

*Do you fear leaving the house?* No. I get bored if I am home for too long.

*How many times per day do you think about germs?* I think about germs after I use the bathroom, which is normal, right?

"Mom, these questions are crazy. I am here for hair pulling, not any of these other weird things."

Now thinking back, many of the measures and questionnaires I was asked to complete are forms I currently use regularly in practice. I find it rather ironic that my first exposure to commonplace psychology assessment tools, was so many years ago when I was the patient!

My father drove from his work to meet us at the center. He arrived promptly before we met the psychiatrist, who was also the director of the office. Dr. T was both a prescriber of medication and a licensed clinical social worker. My parents and I were called back to meet with the doctor. We asked a lot of questions with the most pressing being, "Does medication work for this disorder?" At that time, results of clinical psychopharmacological trials for Trichotillomania were a mixed bag. There was much stronger evidence to suggest that medication would help more with other Obsessive Compulsive Disorder behaviors than Trichotillomania. Inositol was brought to the doctor's attention and unfortunately, he said he was not educated enough on the vitamin to agree or disagree on its use. For the time being, given that I was in my height of puberty, my parents decided to hold off on prescription medication options and focus on Inositol.

Next, we met with a therapist named Nancy in the same office building. She reviewed the forms I had completed in the waiting area and discussed the treatment plan for my presenting problems. The exchange between my parents and Nancy centered upon describing my personality, as if it needed some altering. My father began the conversation.

"Nancy, you see, Lindsey is very…how do I say this…she is a perfectionist. She is always incredibly hard on herself and places expectations that not a single person I know could fulfill. As her parents, we certainly never put this type of pressure on her. This is not how we have raised our children, so I really do not understand where her idea to be faultless and flawless began. As her father, it is very hard to sit back and watch her pull out her hair and be so hard on herself."

My mother imparted her perspective as she became teary-eyed.

"Yes, exactly. I just wish she would love herself more. It hurts me as her mother to see her destroying herself and her beautiful body. She has a history of nail biting and skin picking since she was a little girl. There has always been some behavior present, almost as if she is punishing herself? I don't know. It seems like she is just so unhappy and hates herself or something. I think it is because she is striving for something she will never be able to get and then beats herself up."

Nancy assured my parents and me that these traits and thoughts were commonly seen with Trichotillomania, based upon her experience.

The remainder of the session was spent creating treatment goals. We agreed that I would meet the therapist once a week. Nancy presented me with another chart for daily completion until the next session, which would take place in one week. I was asked to identify the settings of when I pull my hair, the time of day, and what I may be thinking or feeling during this experience. There were two purposes for this exercise. One, this would provide information to the therapist as to emotional and environmental triggers while also gaining an understanding of my frame of reference; and two, self-awareness would be forced upon me as I would need to start paying attention to my thoughts, feelings, and actions. Hopefully, the benefit of self-monitoring would be that I would reduce my pulling behavior. I completed the homework nightly as instructed, because I wanted to be seen as a responsible patient, and I also wanted to get better. Part two of my treatment plan had begun.

Through the rest of my middle school years, my hair pulling remained consistent. My behavior would wax and wane, but the peaks were no higher than the time before and the lulls never lasted more than two days. Despite the peculiar taste of Inositol, I mixed the chalky substance with water to drink every evening before bed. Once I had completed the bottle, I discontinued the treatment, which my parents agreed to, as I did not see any difference on or off Inositol. I felt annoyance toward the therapy homework because I already had so much to do to keep A's in school.

Through eighth grade I persisted with weekly therapy but gradually convinced my parents that it really was not helping either. I had dedicated a full year to therapy and while Nancy seemed very good at what she did, and had supposedly (according to what she said) helped a lot of teenagers like myself, my pulling was stagnant. I remember thinking that the therapy was creating even more temptation to pull since we continued to focus in on the behavior. I reached a point where I thought that perhaps if I did not think about Trichotillomania so much, I would not do it as much. Therapy came to an end.

My entire eighth grade year was spent wearing headbands. Fortunately, just like my experience as a skin picked child, I was never questioned by classmates as to why I suddenly began wearing a headband every day, whether it was in the classroom or on the soccer field. It just goes to show that my looks were not as important to everyone else as they were to me. Nonetheless, I continued to attract the attention of the boys but was not interested in dating. Like therapy and Inositol, I grew tired of headbands and was convinced that it did not help either.

One aspect of Trichotillomania, which always bothered me, left me feeling alone and jealous, was the constant reminder that my girlfriends could alter their hairstyles. I felt cornered into wearing headbands and hairspray every day, yet I so badly wanted to part my hair this way or that. To some, this may not seem like a big deal, but for years this was a huge problem for me.

Take a moment to think of the notoriety that follows a celebrity after a hair change. Many times, hair colors, cuts, and styles are more resounding than accomplishments. This is sad but true. Our society is largely driven by external appearance.

I used to sit in class and watch my friend take her hair down from a ponytail and redo it. I so badly longed to be able to do something as simple as that. It was one form of liberation I was not experiencing. One time, my girlfriend, Jennifer, arrived to school with a new haircut. She was definitely the most popular girl for the day and within the following week, three other friends cut their hair to match hers. I did not have that kind of prerogative to choose how I wanted to wear my hair. The only change I was able to make was not one that I would have chosen for myself but one that made sense from a concealment standpoint. I replaced my headband with bangs cut to the tops of my eyebrows. By using my own hair, I was able to let the bangs cover over my awkward hairline as it was growing in. I despised my bangs as they were a nuisance and made me look younger.

I kept my bangs for the majority of the school year until the hair follicles underneath perked up enough to be able to push back my one-inch forehead spikes of new growth with a trendier version of the cloth headband. As much as having a spiky one inch hairline would be embarrassing and inconvenient for any woman, such a vision was exciting for me. This area was my original pulling site, and I often feared what the long-term ramifications would be. I was thankful that at least I did not damage the hair follicles enough to stunt growth.

# 13

During my time spent in therapy, I was able to identify the environments, which were most favorable for hair pulling. I never touched my hair when I was around others. This included time during the school day or at home in the same room as family members. It is not often that adults with Trichotillomania would feel comfortable in pulling while among other people. I have had patients that became comfortable enough to entertain the idea, but this is not typical for most hair pullers. Conversely, with the younger population, children are more likely to engage in the behavior irrespective of whether company is present. This may not be as surprising given a normal level of impulsivity in early development. Researchers have stated that self-regulation does not develop until the third or fourth year of life. Self-regulation as it relates to impulsivity includes thought processes like thinking before acting, and engaging in fun or pleasurable activity without regard for consequences. Like myself, individuals who pull tend to act before thinking and engage in the pleasurable pulling activity even if the consequence is baldness or feelings of embarrassment and shame.

In my own life, I engaged in the behavior when I was either studying in bed or at the table, on the phone, or on the computer. In my parent's house, the large desktop computer sat on the desk in the kitchen/dining area of the house, which was in a common space. I naturally came to pair the act of reaching my fingers to my hair with sitting at the computer, similar to reaching a hotdog to your mouth while sitting at a baseball game. It was always a challenge to pull sitting at the computer, but I managed well. I would simultaneously work online while listening intently for footsteps approaching toward the kitchen area. Over my years with the disorder, there were countless times in which I was very close to getting caught. Often, I had a kind of *lump in my throat* sensation due to the thought that I was on the verge of getting in trouble. This only added to my stress and anxiety, which likely gave unconscious nourishment to my behavior.

Aside from attempts to deter getting caught mid-act, an additional difficulty in my life was finding the time to clean up my hair. Typically, the scenario would unravel as follows. I would plant myself in front of the computer after school and pull away while alone in the room. Around dinnertime, my mother would enter to begin cooking. Then, I would transition from my computer time to helping with the food preparations. Imagine my feeling of nervousness knowing that I was asked to step away from the computer while leaving behind sometimes hundreds of strands lying on the black keyboard, desktop, chair, and surrounding floor area. Situations like this would often arise in my everyday life. It was unsettling to say the least.

I created so much additional tension in my own life by pulling my hair. I learned to become sneaky to circumvent times like this. If I was in the middle of setting the table and my father entered into the kitchen and approached the computer, I would swoop in like a hawk attacking his prey.

"No dad, I am still working on there."

I learned to be assertive and think quickly. Such statements were never that believable when I was standing in front of him with a stack of china and silverware in my hands.

"I just took a quick break to set the table, but I am getting right back on the computer after this."

I lied a lot because I had to. I felt a lot of guilt as a result. If only I could have said what was actually happening. "Stay clear of the computer desk. My hair is scattered everywhere, and I need to clean it up so no one sees it. Once I have eliminated the mounds of hair, then you are more than welcome to use the computer." Who would be receptive and accepting of such an explanation?

As hard as I tried to maintain a collected composure, most evenings I was a ball of nerves. Further, my attempt to keep things smooth eventually backfired. One late afternoon when I was sitting and pulling in front of the computer, my father walked in from the other room and caught me with my hand to my hair.

"Lindsey, I want you to go upstairs and put something on your head now. I don't care what it is - a bandana, a hat, it doesn't matter. From now on when you are sitting at that computer desk you are to keep something on your head at all times."

My face turned red, and I felt humiliated. Not only was I exposed at that moment, I also did not have the opportunity to clean up my mess before going upstairs to get a bandana. I tied the handkerchief securely around my hair to cover the entire front and crown of my scalp and went back downstairs. This gave my father time to see how much hair was scattered on and around the computer desk.

For the next four years living at home, it became routine to wear a bandana while sitting at the computer. This was to serve as a reminder when I went to touch my scalp that there was a barrier, and I should stop. It became more annoying than anything.

"Get something on your head, Lindsey." This was my constant reminder. I typically responded with an eye roll, a sulk, and a trip upstairs to get a bandana.

What also irritated me was when I was having a good night, which meant a pull-free night, they still reminded me to put something on my head. This led to feelings of frustration and anger. I thought that I was being scolded and inconvenienced whether I was doing something right or wrong. In actuality, my parents were trying to help. Everything they did in these situations was correct and beneficial, but at the time I did not like it.

As an advanced hair puller, I found ways to pull around the bandana. I either slipped my hand under to reach the crown portion of my head, or I would remove the bandana to pull a few pieces and then reposition the handkerchief upon my head. Wearing a covering did not stop me from pulling my hair, it just made it more difficult.

My hair pulling persevered, but my drive to clean up after myself faded. Some nights I showered after my homework at the computer. Then when I walked downstairs, I was greeted to the kitchen with a generic white paper plate. Sometimes the paper plate sat on the counter waiting for my eyes to catch a glance. At other times, my father would say, "Here you go" and hand it to me. I came to truly fear and panic the sight of white paper plates. It was customary that, given my laidback attempts to clean up the hair from around and on the computer desk, my father would grab a white paper plate from the cabinet when I left the kitchen area to shower. He would walk with the paper plate in hand to the computer desk area, and collect each piece of hair from the floor, desk chair, desk surface, and keyboard to pile onto the plate. This was his way of letting me know that he knew I had been pulling, and also to elicit my awareness toward what I had done.

My father was hoping that such a tactic would provide motivation to stop once I had seen all the hair I had removed. I did not like being caught. Some nights I would venture downstairs late at night to talk to friends on Instant Messenger (back in the days of AOL) or to finish writing a school paper. While I had unlimited amounts of time to clean up afterwards, the evening lighting was never conducive to my ability to see each strand of hair. My parents were the first ones downstairs in the morning and, consequentially, I was typically greeted not with coffee or tea but with a white paper plate. I moved out of my parent's house years ago when I left for college and since then, I have not invested in a single pack of white paper plates.

# 14

Trichotillomania definitely has its highs and lows. Some days I would pull less than others without an understanding of why. I often experienced two to three days at a time where I might not have the urge to pull or might feel enough control to not succumb to the urge. After an almost pull-free duration, I would grow confident in my ability to overcome the disorder. As a result, I would stop wearing something on my head and feel half-hearted toward implementing any strategies to resist the pull. It was later that year at a conference that I was told something I will never forget.

"You are never recovered, only in recovery. As soon as you take the mindset that you are recovered, you believe you are safe. You are not. This is when relapse occurs because all skills and strategies you have been using for success are stopped, and you are no longer on-guard toward the disorder. It will win."

I share this with every patient I treat. Personally, those words were life changing.

Through researching, my parents discovered an organization dedicated to Trichotillomania called the *Trichotillomania Learning Center (TLC)*. The *TLC* website serves as an excellent resource for ongoing research, journal articles, treatment providers, personal narrations, and organized events such as workshops, groups, and their annual conference. Fortunately, timing worked in our favor as the deadline to register for the annual weekend conference was approaching. The selected location for the conference that year happened to be nearby in Orlando, Florida which was a blessing, as it could have been hosted anywhere in the country. My parents shared the information with me one night over dinner and they were adamant about our attendance for the entire three-day convention. We registered that night.

We planned to attend the entire weekend, from the welcome session to the closing session. The conference was held at a hotel convention center where there was an abundance of space for the various seminars and workshops as well as adequate hotel rooms for the attendants. The *TLC* conference is comprised of clinicians, researchers, patients, families of patients, and psychology graduate students furthering their knowledge.

Prior to our arrival, we received an extensive information packet inclusive of travel information, hotel arrangements, schedules, descriptions of seminars and workshops, information on the presenters, and current research studies being conducted which we could take part in during the conference. Some of the sessions were held in isolation so everyone could attend; however, most of the sessions were held concurrently and therefore we were required to predetermine which workshops and seminars to attend. The conference offered workshop topics on all of the following: strengthening clinical skills for clinicians, parenting skills and strategies when interacting with a child or teen with Trichotillomania, groundbreaking research studies and results, learning relaxation techniques, and supportive group sessions. My parents and I decided that the more information we could depart with the better. In turn, we agreed to separate after community breakfast each morning. Our strategy sufficed. We each took notes during our respective workshops. In the evening, upon returning to our hotel room after community dinner, we discussed what was learned that day.

In addition to the life changing, unforgettable words which I heard at the conference (as I had mentioned), the experience of the conference itself was moving. I felt anxious and nervous during the four and a half hour car ride to Orlando. Neither my parents nor I knew what to expect. Upon entering the hotel, the entire visual panoramic was that of men and women, boys and girls, of all different ages at various stages of the disorder. This was utterly horrifying and upsetting to the three of us, for I was nowhere near as advanced in the damage I had done to myself. At this point in my life, I had several bald patches, each no larger than the diameter of a quarter and somewhat disguisable. To my eyes, the *TLC* conference looked more like a cancer convention. Women walked around with shaved heads, and absence of eyebrows and eyelashes. Children lacking the same facial features joyfully played together. It appeared as though those who were not bald had full wigs. I saw more people that fit such a descriptive than those who looked like I did. I felt unsettled at the sight of so many children without eyelashes and eyebrows. Never in my life had I seen that before, and it took almost the whole weekend to get accustomed to seeing it.

Aside from the rich information gained from the weekend, three particular feelings resonated. I felt a deep sense of gratitude for not having reached the point that many other hair pullers had. Making such comparisons really put my own behaviors into perspective as I recognized that my problem could always be worse. I also felt immense, immeasurable hope and motivation to stop due to the fear of the severity of the disorder and in hearing the success stories of those who had overcome Trichotillomania. My parents agreed that they did not know how bad such a disorder could become.

The last feeling I departed with was that of acceptance by others. The conference was the first time in which I did not feel alone in my disorder. There were countless other individuals who felt the same during that weekend. There are no words to describe what it was like to meet others who had suffered as I had. It seemed as though all of these children and adults, who had gone to great lengths to conceal their hair issues, were finally given an opportunity in a safe environment to bare their souls. Although I did not experience teasing as a child, I knew that all of the children at the conference were vying for acceptance and understanding from other children. The conference was a safe space—an opportunity and an outlet to be themselves.

On the last day of the conference, before the attendees went their separate ways, it was announced that a situation had occurred the night before. The children of the conference had united. The night before, approximately 40 children had stripped themselves of their wigs, hats, bandanas, and hair attachments in front of each other and jumped in the hotel pool with shouts of happiness, acceptance, and liberation. This was the most touching part of the entire weekend. I took a moment to reflect upon my own life, how I shared a similar desire to be free and accepted at the deepest part of my core.

It has been approximately fourteen years since my first conference, and I still keep the handouts, notes, and worksheets in my possession. While the pages are yellow and dusty, and the information is outdated due to the exceptional research in the field, I glance at the notes every now and then. This serves as a reminder of how much the field of psychology has progressed, how my own knowledge and understanding has remarkably advanced, and how far I have come in my personal experience with the disorder and in life.

# 15

I returned from the *TLC* conference with a renewed perspective on my disorder and my life. This happens quite often when an individual seeks an opportunity, such as a meditation retreat, religious conference, or missionary work. We leave the experience with something new and different than that with which we arrived. For some it is captivating stories, for others it is exquisite photography. Nonetheless, the stories and photos do not account for the personal transformation that, sometimes, cannot be expressed with language. I toiled with how to make those feelings last, the feelings of passion, motivation, and determination to continue on my new path toward self-enhancement and growth.

The novelty and richness of my experience gradually faded and after remaining pull free for two months post-conference (which was the longest I had gone without pulling), I found myself sliding back into my old ways. At the time, I was not able to identify what thoughts were associated with this decision, for it was certainly not something I had set out to do. Emotionally, I felt disgruntled. The reality is that a short-lived conference did not have the ability to make the long-lasting changes necessary in my life. It was just an additional tool, which merely provided support, references, and clarity to what I was doing and why I should stop. I was the only person stopping me from breaking free of Trichotillomania, and I was the only person that could make the decision to implement change. It was not until entering high school, with partially grown out bangs, and a few thinned, nickel-sized areas on my crown, that I truly made that decision.

My behavior had persisted for at least two years at this point. I had therapy, Inositol, the *TLC* conference, parental support, and environmental deterrents in my past. In my future, I had endless opportunity, and my life was mine to seize. The high school years were vastly different as compared to middle school. My life revolved around my social schedule both in and out of school. Guys and girls were starting to form real relationships, and I discovered my first crush. I had been in school with him since the start of middle school, but apparently it took some time for puberty and my hormones to get up to speed. My first love, although he did not know it at the time, was strong motivation to take my hair growth to the next level. Additionally, I secured positions on the varsity cheerleading squad, varsity soccer team, and varsity tennis team, which meant that I would be performing for some very important male spectators. During the school day, I spent much of my time speaking in front of peers, given that I was class president, on the debate team, and an officer in the honor society. I also took part in school plays, albeit small roles where I stood in the background.

My social status, my reputation, my extracurricular involvement, and the hope of winning over my crush enabled

Trichotillomania to find a subordinate place in my life. My priorities were different, and I was unavailable for my disorder. I wanted to remain known as the girl with the gorgeous hair, not the girl with bald patches.

As a safeguard, I sought the help from a new therapist close to my school named Ann. At this time, I was able to drive myself to my therapist's office. I felt a greater sense of responsibility for my time spent in therapy than in the previous years, given that I was taking myself to and from appointments. This occurred on my own time and at my willingness, not anyone else's. My parents continued to support my treatment endeavors.

"Was it a good day or a bad day?" my father asked each night.

His inquiry was in reference to my pulling. This was his way of supporting me and letting me know that he was willing to remain by my side throughout my journey with Trichotillomania. I felt encouraged. My mother was always willing to attend therapy; I just needed to say the magic words. As my parents came to realize that I was trying to grasp my own life challenges, they remained present but were not overwhelming. This transition allowed me to focus on what I needed to do to help myself, rather than what they were doing to help me. My thoughts centered on the understanding that I was now too old for punishment or lectures for my repetitive behaviors. This provided the space where I felt safe enough to actually be honest and let them know when I was struggling or when I had gone several days pull-free. We were able to sympathize or rejoice, respectively.

As it relates to the classroom setting, concern for how my hair looked was always my biggest problem in school. My thoughts were always divided between attention to the class material and concern that part of my hair had become exposed for those behind me to stare. My divided attention would alert me when an area was exposed. The parts of my scalp with minimal or absence of hair tended to be very sensitive to cool temperatures. I was easily able to feel a breeze or air conditioning on my bald or balding spots because these areas were devoid of hair, where we have lots of nerve endings. Fortunately, my grades were not affected by such a distraction.

In the mornings, I would spend ample time with various creams, gels, and hairsprays to position my existing hair over the patchy areas in order to prevent detection. This required a great deal of my time and meticulousness. I needed several mirrors including a hand mirror. I would turn my back to my vanity mirror and then hold the hand mirror in front of my face to see what the back of my hair looked like. I also gave attention to the sides. It truly was exasperating morning after morning.

Once my front and back hairline had grown in by the start of ninth grade, my problem area became my crown. Through self-exploration, I found various sensitive spots on my crown region, which provided the largest tactile reinforcement, and I continued to revisit those places. In the mornings, I would typically take the front section back to cover the crown and then secure it in place with a band or clip. The lower half of my hair would hang down to touch my shoulders. It was a *half-up, half-down* hairstyle. Once the front section was secured in place, I then spent a lot of time with the placement of individual pieces. I needed to spread out the top layer across my entire scalp and hold firm with hairspray and gel. I also paid attention to how much hair was allocated to cover each part of my scalp. Further, a rocky day's forecast which included strong winds or rain, enough to concern any female with her hair, was always bad news and a guaranteed *bad hair day.*

The phrase *bad hair day* makes me laugh because although most take it figuratively, in my life it was the literal truth. Out of curiosity, I wish I had tracked my expenditure of hair products over the years. For the time being, I was at least fortunate to have my own hair to hold in place, even if it was not the exact look I desired.

One school experience, in particular, resonates in my memory. I was sitting in my natural sciences class. The classroom was laid out so the desks were in rows with the back of each chair touching the front lip of the desk behind it. In other words, the desks were sandwiched together, and we all sat very close to one another. I sat in the row second from the left about half way back from the dry erase board, which hung at the head of the classroom. We had assigned seats. I sat between Jay, who was in front of me, and Cory, who was behind me. I was deep into writing lecture notes in my binder about friction and velocity when I felt fingers in my hair. They were not mine.

Cory had reached her arm forward, for reasons unknown to me, and stroked a piece of hair protruding from the center of my crown. In this very place was a three-inch piece of hair, about one-half inch wide, which was in its growing phase. It happened to be the most sensitive, pleasurable location on all of my head, and it only took me three years of pulling to discover. The little spike always caused me the most trouble in the morning because it was in the phase where it was too short to lay down flat but too long to let stand up. I applied a thick gelatinous lather directly to the spike to glue it down to my other existing hair. Sometimes, the gel would dry on the hair creating a rigid spike, but it would not keep the hair securely fastened, which was my exact experience that day.

I quickly smacked my hand to the back of my head, similar to what you do when trying to catch a fly between your hand and a wall. I felt my face turn bright red and the familiar pit-like feeling returned to my stomach in one breath. I turned around and Cory was smiling and laughing to herself.

"Ha ha. What is that? You have a little baby *spikey* there. Let me see." She tried to playfully move my hand away.

"Cory, no. Stop."

I took some of my heavier hair and shifted it over the firm gelled piece, hoping to keep it tacked. I was humiliated and angry.

For the remainder of the class period, my hair was the only thing on my mind.

A week later, I arrived to school ten minutes before the first period bell rang. The student body waited downstairs in the outside courtyard to congregate and converse. Cory approached and commented about my hair, even without a visible reminder.

"How is your little *spikey* doing? Let me see it."

Cory was one of the tallest girls in our grade, and in this situation, her height worked to her advantage as she was able to peer over my head and glance at my crown without my having to turn around.

"I haven't seen it this past week in natural sciences. What happened to it?"

I had never met anyone, aside from Cory, that was so into probing and prodding into a place she did not belong.

"Whatever, Cory. Please just drop it. It's covered, okay?"

Two days later, on a Friday, I was walking from the academic building to the cafeteria when I heard Cory again, who was walking with her best friend, Karen.

"I see it! Karen, look! Lindsey has a little piece of hair shorter than the rest. Isn't it cute?"

Now there were two people who were focused on my scalp. "Great, word will be out on this before the end of the day now that they both see it," I thought to myself. Cute was certainly the last adjective on my mind when thinking about Trichotillomania.

If they only knew! I felt my mind begin to race with excuses and responses. "Say something, Lindsey! Anything…" I thought to myself, and out spewed a beautiful lie.

"My youngest brother was goofing around with his friend. Last week they were blowing bubbles with their chewing gum and, well, it ended up in my hair. Let's just say that it will be another month before I speak to either of them."

That was the best I could do for being put on the spot. They took the bait. Karen said,

"No way. You have got to be f'n with me. He seriously popped gum in your hair and you had to cut it out?"

"No. I didn't have to cut my hair. My mom did. It was in a place too hard for me to reach. I flipped out and was too emotional to use scissors that close to my head."

We all started laughing but for different reasons. My laughter was the nervous kind of laugh, like when on a first date and there's an awkward silence and you laugh. They found entertainment value in my suffering.

The experience of knowing someone is sitting right behind me staring at the back of my head creates heightened awareness and is very distracting. Unfortunately, this is a natural part of life as long as I am surrounded by people. I will always have movie goers sitting in the rows behind me. Unless I purchase tickets for the last row of a concert, I will always have music fans staring at my head and the stage. Organized workshops or classrooms will undoubtedly have desks in rows. It was distracting then, and it still is now, even with nothing to cover. This is the result of living through so many years of heightened awareness and concern for the appearance of my hair.

# 16

Ann's office was conveniently located near my private high school. The office building was made from old brown wood and looked a bit haggard. The therapy suite was quaint, with a small waiting area and two therapy rooms. The waiting area was warm and inviting, as if I were sitting in the living room of an acquaintance's house. There were dimly lit lamps, magazines, a box of tissues on the coffee table, a sofa, and a large recliner with ottoman. It had been quite the departure from my days at Dr. Fred's bungalow. It only took close to ten years to find an office equipped with magazines that I actually enjoyed. I sat in the waiting room in my school uniform and read *Vogue*.

I had feelings of confidence rather than nervousness. This was due to the fact that I had been to two different therapists and a psychiatrist, and because I had stopped pulling since finalizing my appointment with Ann two weeks prior. I figured that if I led into the therapy session with that fact, she would be able to tell me I was an amazing patient and full of motivation before we even started treatment. I also wanted to make sure she knew I was experienced in the therapeutic process and presented with a sound box of skills to aid in the cause. I was also a bit excited that I would finally have the chance to begin with a clean slate and tell her about myself, in contrast to entering into therapy after my parents had conveyed their perspective on my life and my situation. Ann was in her mid sixties with curly brown hair. She had rosy plump cheeks to match her stout build. She seemed to be a happy lady, and resembled one of my own relatives, which helped me to feel like I knew her a little better, despite it being our very first session.

The first session was spent building rapport and achieving a level of comfort to where I could share my thoughts and feelings with Ann. Aside from my response to the reason for presenting to therapy, the word *hair* was not mentioned. I appreciated that Ann had recognized me for more than my disorder. The fifty-minute session was speedy. We ended with the understanding of how the therapy process would proceed and a statement of treatment goals. We scheduled my second session for the following Wednesday after school.

At the time I started to see Ann, a family member began frequenting a hypnotherapist bi-weekly to address a very different problem. My parents presented the idea of hypnosis to my list of choices, and I decided I would first research to make sure that it made sense for my given problem.

Hypnosis is used to elicit change in a patient's thoughts, feelings, or actions through accessing the subconscious. My perspective on hypnosis at the time was that it was *pseudo-science*; it was *hokey*, and on television they put people into a trance state to do entertaining things. Some of my opinions were very similar to people not fully informed through direct experiences with hypnosis in an educational program, or personal exposure to a hypnotherapist. I had stereotypes and prejudices about the practice and about what hypnotherapists look like. I always imagined a lady in a long flowing gown with a crystal ball that engaged in astrology and palm reading. My thought was also that working more exclusively with meditative practices was superior. People tend to judge that which they do not know, and I too am guilty. According to a research article by John Khilstrom of the University of California, Berkeley, hypnosis has many benefits on thought, including increasing memory, gaining control over mental processing, decreasing closed mindedness, and *deautomatizing* automatic processes.

If it were not for the success I saw from my family member who visited Flo, short for Florence, I may not have ever tried hypnosis. Insurance typically does not cover what they consider to be alternative therapies or alternative treatments, which includes hypnosis. My parents were willing to do anything to help me, so they agreed to pay for several sessions out of pocket, and I agreed to give it a try. I visited Flo for the first time two days after my first therapy session with Ann. Flo worked out of her home. The interior of the house looked exactly like I had pictured a hypnotherapist's house in my mind. It was eccentric, as was she. The house was stuffy and cluttered. The walls were coated with vibrant *old Florida* scenes of pink flamingoes on the beach. Life sized pink flamingo statues were dispersed throughout the home. The full length of the wall in Flo's living room looked like a Bedazzler machine (the flimsy, plastic machine from the 80's that punched rhinestones into fabric) had gotten busy. I am thankful that I did not judge Flo's hypnotic abilities on her home environment, for I would have thought she was lacking direction. She was a bit scattered but incredibly sweet, kindhearted, and invested in helping me achieve my goals.

There was a separate den at the front of her house, which she claimed to be the treatment room. In the den was a desk, a large recliner chair, and a black, bulky cassette tape/CD player with a microphone attached. The room was rather stuffy like the rest of the house, but her ceiling fan helped the situation. There was question as to whether I would have the ability to be *brought under* given my strong will and intellect, according to Flo. I believe almost anyone can experience hypnosis if given the ability to relax, for it is a form of mental relaxation.

Flo asked me to sit in the oversized, cloth recliner placed in the corner of the room near a window. She offered minimal words to prepare me for the session. I felt very nervous but was reminded that my family member had great success in working with her and therefore, I probably would as well.

"Close your eyes, and relax. Begin to take some deep breaths. Today, we are going to do something very special which will bring you great benefit."

I was convinced that my ability to achieve a state of deep relaxation was due to Flo's voice. The vocal tone of a hypnotherapist is the key. She spoke with soft and polite gestures - that of a voice you would hear on a children's lullaby. A transcendental, instrumental melody filled the room as Flo spoke into the microphone and began to count backward from ten. She was recording this session for later use.

"Ten…you are becoming relaxed, nine, eight, seven, deeper and deeper you are going into a relaxed state, six, five, oh so happy and so relaxed, four, three, we are on our way to a happy place, two, one…"

The following things I recall from my transcendental session with Flo. She took me on a journey where I went through doorways, into a forest, looked at the illuminating cheerful sun, and found my stop color of red. Flo did a color-word association while I was on my journey to pair the vision of red with the thought of stopping my hair pulling. The result of this meant that when I was back in my normal state of consciousness, I would be reminded to stop pulling when I saw the color red anywhere in my environment. During my hypnotic experience, Flo also discussed bright, white, healthy light entering into my body while cloudy, dim light exited with each passing inhalation and exhalation. At the end of my hypnosis, Flo counted from one to ten as I was slowly reawakened and opened my eyes. The feeling after this session was similar to waking up after a massage in a spa; relaxed, tired, content, and purged of toxins. I left the session with my personalized CD and was instructed to listen to it nightly. We scheduled the next session for one week later.

Between the weekly hypnosis and the weekly therapy sessions, I remained level. The Trichotillomania was neither worse nor better over the subsequent year. I consistently saw both Ann and Flo and did what I was told but was unable to make it past five days pull-free. Fortunately, the days when I was pulling my hair did not amount to enough damage to cause new bald patches. Therefore, I was able to complete my tenth grade year successfully with my own hair, which I could wear up or down as long as I applied the right products.

While the hypnosis sessions were relaxing, the therapy sessions were utterly exhausting. My expectations were anything other than the reality of how draining it feels to self-explore and self-analyze. Some people may view mental health therapy as being necessary for those who are weak-minded individuals; I have heard that from previous patients. This opinion on therapy, changes after having experienced the emotional release first-hand. The time spent with my therapist felt overwhelming, rewarding, and challenging, and I always slept well the night after a therapy session. Sometimes, I would come home from therapy and be in an unintentional short, snappy, moody mental state. In review, this is actually a good sign for it means that I was working hard on myself to the point of depletion, like when the candle has been burned at both ends, and I crave sleep. I often felt that way after therapy.

From attending therapy alone with Ann, I was able to gain my own understanding as to how I functioned as an individual. It was no coincidence that Ann helped me to uncover the same personality facets that my parents had discussed with Nancy years prior. The only difference is that years before, it seemed like my parents and therapist was teaming against me because I was not as committed to therapy. In hindsight, I can partially, almost fully, agree with their opinions. I would not agree with my parent's perspective that I ever hated myself, but I certainly did feel anger toward how I looked. Further, I wanted to be the best in all areas of my life. My definition of *the best*, however, was perfection. I wanted to be stellar at all times, no excuses. I was in competition with myself every day. Taking the time to analyze my life and myself led to identification of some of my unstated, unwritten expectations. If I were to write them down, they would include:

1) taking advantage of every extracurricular opportunity I qualified for such as clubs, volunteer work, sports, and organizations;

2) completing every honors and Advanced Placement (AP) course that my school offered;

3) earning over a 4.0 grade point average

in high school, which was made possible through the additional weight of honors and AP courses;

4) being popular which would require every classmate to consider me a friend;

5) making sure all the teachers and faculty liked me;

6) keeping a clean bedroom at all times; maintaining a consistent, year-round tan;

7) upholding a facial regimen to prevent any acne (despite having poor skin genetics);

8) never getting in trouble with my parents;

9) never drinking or trying any recreational drugs;

10) never saying profanity; and

11) helping around the house without being asked.

I feel exhausted reading the list. Is there anyone able to maintain such nonsensical expectations all the time?

# 17

I celebrated my one-year therapy anniversary, by terminating treatment. I gained an in-depth analysis and understanding of who I was as a person and what my unconscious had carried around for many years. Between the talk therapy with Ann and hypnosis with Flo, I again grew confident that I knew exactly what I needed to do to stop my *BFRB*. I was incredibly wrong. It is all too often that a patient terminates therapy prematurely. It is usually around the time that he or she is on the brink of a major breakthrough or has just overcome an obstacle. We do amazing things to prove to the self that we are strong and capable, and then gradually revert back to old lifestyles when we no longer continue to implement the appropriate change. Then when the problem returns, we wonder what happened. We are not invincible.

My junior year of high school is when my hair pulling really headed south on a one-way ticket. The areas of my crown, which I had pulled, had grown back at various lengths and rates. The new growth was promising and exciting, but the peculiarities in the way my hair looked were embarrassing. There is nothing appealing about a haircut of varying lengths ranging from one half inch to shoulder length. I knew that as the short pieces continued to grow so would my long pieces. Well, there was only one solution to this hairy nightmare. I had to surrender to nature's course, and the clippers, and get a haircut that would reduce the discrepancy between lengths. The result was a horrific haircut that, to me, looked like a mullet, short, choppy layers on top while keeping length in the back. Let's just say I would not have gotten such a cut were I paid on a dare. I cried leaving the salon that day. I could have reminded myself it was just hair that would grow back, but I could not overlook the fact that such an atrocious appearance would be something I would have to look at on a daily basis for many months. I was devastated.

The following eight months, I wore my hair *half-up, half-down* tied back with a clip. My scalp seemed to become more sensitive, in a satisfying way, and therefore my pulling worsened. I still only pulled when at home in bed, on the phone, or in front of the computer but I was now working my thumb and pointer finger like each day of pulling were my last. I became very efficient in reaping the satisfying physical feeling in short periods of time. I targeted my crown area and never touched my eyelashes or eyebrows, thankfully. I do not know how I would have been able to conceal more than my scalp if required. That alone was time consuming. My post-pull rituals remained consistent; examining the root, biting off the root, or playing with the strand and then letting it gracefully float to the floor.

Despite my years of therapy, there were only a few associated thoughts during my pull episodes, which I could identify. "Why am I doing this? I should not be doing this. I am going to regret it." Just like the thoughts of many failed or struggling dieters, I took a procrastination-like, black-and-white mindset when I had the moment to step back from my pulling episode and analyze. "There is always tomorrow to start over again. I already blew it for today, so I might as well make it worthwhile and go all out. Then try again tomorrow." What I see as being the primary problem with these thoughts is that I did not simply start over again tomorrow. When a new day approached, I was left with the damages from the day, week, month, and even year before because hair did not grow back as soon as I stopped toiling with it.

In one to two months time, my entire crown consisted of exposed bare scalp and areas of peach fuzz for hair. The hair that I had been pulling back from my face to cover over my scant crown became too thin. What began as a patch the size of a dime soon diffused to cover an area the diameter of a grapefruit, approximately six inches wide. Apparently, I had been as persistent in my mental health disorder success as I had in my academics.

One night, upon stepping from the shower to my vanity after washing my hair, I was reminded of the feelings I had felt the first time I woke up and saw my hairline years ago. At this moment I was glaring at myself in the mirror with sopping hair pouring drops onto my shoulders and chest. It was as if my hair was crying tears of pain and grief over the lost strands. I put a towel over my balding head. My eyes were listless as I sat on my toilet seat to cry. I could not accept that what I saw looking back at me was a ghastly sight of someone who looked like a chemotherapy patient. I became hysterical, and my thoughts were that it would have been an easier pill to swallow if I had been diagnosed with cancer. At least I could blame it on chemotherapy. Chemotherapy is a form of medication known and accepted in society, while Trichotillomania is not. Further, I had no one to blame. I had pulled out each and every strand with my own two hands and had no real reason for doing so other than it passed the time and felt good in the moment.

My parent's bedroom was just a short distance from mine and it was not unusual that they could hear me when I was crying. My mother knocked on my bedroom door and opened it before I could tell her to enter. She found me sitting in my bathroom with the towel still in place. There was nothing I could do besides have a conversation with her and be truthful.

"I need help. I am not ever going to show you what I have done, but I do not know what to do. I have done so much damage that it can no longer be covered." The tears streamed steadily downward.

"I have ruined myself, I have ruined my appearance, and I have made my own life difficult and miserable. Even if I stop pulling tonight, my hair will not grow back tomorrow or even in a week. I have to live with the consequences of my actions for months, or even years."

My mother had a look of solace on her face but gave sound advice.

"This is a little bump in the road. This is a minor setback. You can get through this. You know what you need to do. Beating yourself up over the situation is not going to help anything. Tomorrow is a new day." She pulled me to my feet and hugged me.

"No one said this was going to be easy, and you will fight through this. I promise."

I had no understanding as to why she was confident when I was not. My mother believed in me when I did not believe in myself.

"Your father and I heard you crying. Is it okay if I go tell him what happened?"

I agreed, and my mother departed for approximately twenty minutes. During that time, I found a bandana and securely attached it to my soaking wet head. I lacked motivation to dry my hair. I was afraid to touch or brush my hair for fear of losing even more hair. If only my fear could last indefinitely.

Thirty minutes later my mother returned.

"Your father and I were talking. We both realize how difficult this is for you and know that you have been trying by listening to your CD at night and attending therapy. It also makes me happy to see that you have a bandana on your head to prevent you from pulling. I was thinking, would you like to meet me at the flea market tomorrow to look for a hairpiece? They have all kinds of pieces with different attachments, some with real hair. I would suggest we find you a nice full piece made from real hair that closely matches your own. We can also take it to the salon to have your colorist match your hair and the piece. No one will be able to tell the difference. These days there are a lot of women wearing extensions and hair attachments."

I did not know what to say. I was opposed to getting a hairpiece because all I could visualize was a full wig that a woman with a bald head would wear. However, I was not against the idea enough to disagree with my mother's invitation because I could not think of a better alternative. I pushed my ego aside and agreed.

The following morning, I dressed for school as usual and tied my hair back in a ponytail with the aid of hairspray. My mullet-inspired haircut prevented an easy ponytail from forming, so I had to secure shortened pieces with hairspray and bobby pins. During my school day, I continuously reflected upon how my appearance had gone down the drain due to my disorder.

In reality, this was my perfectionism getting the best of me in realizing that I could not meet the unstated expectation of wanting to look perfect all the time. I was learning the hard way that I would soon have to throw my unconscious desires far away, out of sight. It was also during that school day that I decided I could not go swimming in my backyard pool or the ocean with company. Water was no longer my friend. I could not ride in a car with the windows open or top down. The wind did not agree with me. I could not engage in sports where I broke a sweat unless I had a bandana or an alternate head garment covering. Sweat was an enemy. I stopped planning and attending sleepovers because I feared shifting around on my pillow during the night and waking up with an unsightly area exposed. Fun now had its limitations. There was no way I was going to become romantically involved with anyone as all I could imagine was my hairpiece being pulled off or a hand reaching to my hair and feeling something off-putting. I had officially lost my freedom to have fun, to look how I wanted to look, and to experience romantic love. Trichotillomania had put its foot down as if to say, "I am in charge now." I was imprisoned by my own impulsive desires. It was so not worth it!

I have watched television series about substance abuse; the story of an individual that gradually finds his way to drugs and alcohol and is convinced that he does not have a problem. He continues to do things his way until one day reality punches him square in the face. At that point he is deep in the hole, in darkness, in a cold dreary place where he is alone. You never want to be that far in when you decide to have the motivation to pull yourself back out. It takes twice as much energy and willpower to undo what you have done. It is not impossible but requires tenacity and grit. Just like my wish for the continued motivation and renewal after an enlightening conference, I too wished that the feelings of hitting rock bottom would be a sound reminder to never slide back down the hole.

For the individual who has never fought through a mental health disorder, the best parallel is the day you wake up and realize you are turning 30, 40, 50, 60, or 70 years old. You question what happened to the time. I experienced much the same nostalgic feeling, when in the middle of my disorder. Time seemed nonexistent, just an abstract, meaningless concept. Pushing myself outside of my struggles allowed me to realize that I could be more than my behavior. This part of my life consumed an abundance of time, but it was not all of me, nor all of my time, nor all of my life. Why do we have to endure hardships to learn a rich, invaluable lesson?

In 2001, my mother and I walked through the flea market on a hunt for a hairpiece as promised. The flea market was a gargantuan indoor mall with row after row of white tents lined like soldiers in white uniforms creating a walking path for an important official. In this case, the merchandise was much less prestigious. The goods ranged in quality; scarves, sunglasses, lamps, wooden signs, fruit, nail polish, imported clothing, watches, and hairpieces. My nerves got the best of me, as I was more concerned with what the booth attendants at the hairpiece stands, who spoke broken English, would think of a teenage girl shopping for a sizable hairpiece. I would have preferred feeling excited for the opportunity, but the realization that I had turned the corner to hair replacement was flooding my mind with images of old women in wheel chairs and chemotherapy patients. It was daunting to persuade myself that there was nothing here to judge except judgment itself.

Approximately two hours and various hair booths later, we had found a hairpiece. Our first hairpiece purchase was a clip-in piece that I could easily take in and out without assistance. The base was large enough in diameter to cover my crown. It ran from the left side to the right side of my scalp, almost ear to ear, and the length correlated with the longest part of my natural hair. The color could use some help, but that was for the precision of my expert colorist to match and perfect. As much as I had fought against a hairpiece, I felt thankful for securing a piece that provided some type of normalcy. I was more grateful for my parents who devised a practical solution, rather than lecture me on the current state of my hair.

# 18

The clip-in hairpiece, worn daily, bought me some time away from Trichotillomania. It served several purposes including making my mornings run more smoothly. It was a relief to cover the area of hair that I always targeted when pulling, and it provided flexibility on how I styled my hair. I would attach the piece first thing in the morning and leave it in until I was falling asleep, sometimes keeping it in through the night. I tried not to let this happen, as the metal hair clips caused massive amounts of discomfort during the night while sleeping, and the piece itself, although real hair, tended to knot more easily than my own hair. Nonetheless, the piece did its job well. Given that I did not have an easy access to my crown, my hair grew back during my senior year, not just some of it but all of it. Hair growth is always unpredictable. I have heard that hair growth, texture, and thickness change over the years. Some have told me every seven years and others have told me that it is variable. The verdict is still out on this.

When my hair grew in, it was exactly the same as my existing hair. This was miraculous given that I always pulled the entire hair, including shaft and root. Some hair follicles had the pleasure of meeting my fingers more than once, and I was certain that these strands would never again make an appearance. This was not the case, my new hair blended with the old, perhaps even a little bit thicker than my original hair (which was substantial). Each night, I would go into my parent's bedroom to show them how much my hair had grown from the day before. Obviously, my excitement clouded my reality; hair does not change *that* much from day to day but this really did not matter. Each night my parents and I celebrated a small, pull-free victory. Each day meant I was one day closer to having Trichotillomania in the history books. I had also set semi-long term goals for myself with senior prom, high school graduation, and the start of college approaching. The best part was I was doing it on my own. I do not want to discredit the years of therapy, doctors visit, medicine, and hypnosis as these treatment options provided me with guidance and the proper tools to get me to where I had landed.

To this day, it is hard for me to verbalize the feelings in accomplishing something I had been fighting against, and suffering from for so long. Only those who have set what seems to be an unattainable goal and then mastered it would be able to empathize with my feelings. It is an over- the-moon, euphoria that lasts a long, long time. For those who have set a goal that has not been achieved, keep after it. If I can, you can too. If there is something in your way, remove it or rewrite your goal.

On the day of my senior graduation, I walked across the stage with my own hair. Yet my past still followed. I sat in the pews of the church where we had the ceremony. The entire church was filled to capacity with family, friends, and supporters of the class of 2003. Throughout the whole service, an anxious feeling continued to fall upon me, a nice reminder that I had Trichotillomania for so many years. I was worried about the very end of the graduation when we all had to take our caps off and throw them in the air. I thought, *I will take off my hat and be exposed for everyone to see without me first seeing what my hair looks like underneath.* My thought was highly irrational and unrealistic given that I had a full head of hair, but understandable given what I had been through. I was product of my past circumstances. Sadly, due to this fear, I was unable to be fully mentally and emotionally present in the moment of my graduation, a monumental event in my lifetime. I never shared this with anyone.

Going through that time where I had conflicting emotions, and was only partially present, has greatly aided in my ability to relate to patients who have come to therapy to deal with thoughts and feelings of a past situation that are hindering present feelings. While I continuously challenge myself to live in the present moment, I need to also celebrate the Trichotillomania-free pastimes because they were fleeting moments in the grand scheme of life.

I was told college would be a whole new world, full of excitement, challenges, and growth. Whoever told me that was certainly not sharing this news with hair pulling in mind. There was no growth involved with college, as it related to the brown pieces atop my head. Hopefully by now you are starting to see the wax-and-wane, ebb-and-flow of Trichotillomania.

When I submitted for freshman housing at Lehigh University in Pennsylvania, my first choice was a private room in the freshman dorm. This appeared to be the best option, as I would have my own space and privacy but still reside on a female hall with communal bathrooms, and surrounding friends. I received a letter about a month before the start of my freshman year. They had placed me in one of the best dorms and assigned me to a private suite. A private room for a person fighting through Trichotillomania is a nightmare. I had been liberated for several months, but that did not mean I was recovered.

As soon as I moved into my room, my hair pulling came back with a vengeance. Apparently, it was pissed that I had forgotten about it for so many months and was out to prove itself yet again. Having a private room, much like I had at home, meant that I constantly had a nonpublic place to pull anytime my door was closed. Further, I did not have my hairpiece to help deter my fingers. You may be thinking, *'Well, the easy solution is to keep your door open.'* Try telling a person on a diet with a box of cookies, easily accessible and always visible, to put it away and not eat any. The most viable solution is to throw the cookies out, but why doesn't the person do it? It is a challenge and requires motivation. Perhaps you throw away the box of cookies, but then something takes over you as you drive to the grocery store the next day to buy a new box.

I was neither able to throw out my dorm room, nor take the door off the hinges. It became incredibly easy to close my door at all times. If my girlfriends wanted to see me, they knew where to find me. All they had to do was knock. That also meant that I would have to hastily clear away the scattered pieces and attempt to look presentable within seconds. I created a lot of unnecessary stress for myself. I was essentially repeating the past, of living with my parents and having to stay on my toes, all over again. *I need to stop. I am now in college, away from my hairpiece, and away from a hair salon,* I thought. I often viewed my hairpiece like a child views a blanket, safe, and comfortable. It was a great anxiety reducer!

Aside from my feelings of panic and stress, I also recognized that with passing time I was isolating myself because I was pulling more. As a hair puller, two of the worst things for me were when I had unstructured time, and when I had too much time by myself, for both aspects automatically defaulted to my fingers in my hair. Trichotillomania always followed me around and required minimal effort, so I could go back to it no matter what.

The downside of living in a small room was that there were fewer places for my hair to land. I was always living in and around pulled hair. It felt like I was always stuck in a spider web. Every day I would take out my petite red Hoover vacuum to clear my space. This cleanse, while a form of emotional catharsis to purge my previous behavioral sins, only lasted a few hours before I was right back in a pile of hair. I exhausted many vacuum cleaners that year.

My feeling toward the communal bathroom was opposite to the nightmarish experience of having my own dorm room. It was a pleasure to have an unavoidable space where I was always in the presence of one or more females who could prevent me from succumbing to temptation. I was in a constant state of internal struggle. I wanted to be alone, but at the same time I didn't.

Before leaving for college, I worried greatly about how I would wash my hair without others seeing me. This concern worked to my benefit, as I had to wrap my wet hair in a towel before I exited the shower stall. As a result, I was never able to see what my hair looked like while wet, and therefore never became repulsed at the growing site of baldness. I typically walked from the bathroom to my private room to dry my hair and continue with the evening studies or whatever else was planned at the time. Similar to my time spent living at home, I found ways to be sneaky and circumvent getting caught with my *hair down*. None of the girls on my floor ever knew anything about Trichotillomania (not to my knowledge) and I was never questioned.

Like the average college freshman, spring approached with

spring break on my mind. Being that I was from Florida but attending college in Pennsylvania with every other student from the northeast, a few of my friends and I planned to celebrate our first spring break in Florida. It seemed like a great idea at the moment, but I let the excitement of beaches, tanning, clubs, and shopping engulf my logic. Three girlfriends and I made our way to Florida where we shared one hotel room.

Many problems resulted during this trip, all of which would have been nonexistent if I had not had Trichotillomania. First, I had nowhere to hide when it came time to blow dry my hair after a shower. It was my first college spring break and also my first time having to wash, blow dry, and style my hair with three others in the same room. I had never even let my parents see my wet hair. *Think quick, Lindsey*, I told myself while scrambling for a witty suggestion.

"It would probably be best if I dry my hair in the bathroom with the door closed since it takes me a while. It will make the room really hot, and the radio or television will be hard to hear if I am out here with you." Lame but acceptable excuse, I suppose.

My girlfriends accepted the proposition. Nonetheless, the awkwardness, nervousness, and embarrassment I felt was so significant that I still think about the week of my first spring break as an experience, which was more work than delight. In addition to drying my hair in the bathroom, the second problem that arose was swimming. I stayed out of the pool and the ocean despite the nearly 100-degree weather. It took just one day of sitting on the beach in Florida to burn to a crisp. The trip ended with a sunburn and without a conversation about Trichotillomania.

The three girlfriends I brought to Florida were the same three that I decided to live with for our sophomore year. We entered the housing lottery and again, I received my first choice, a spacious, on-campus four-bedroom apartment at the top of the mountain overlooking the University. One week before the sophomore semester began, we reunited to move in and decorate. We had a common area, which consisted of a furnished living room, furnished dining room, kitchen, and bathroom. There were four bedrooms, each the same sized room and closet. The rooms were formulated in a line down a narrow hallway within the apartment.

I returned for sophomore year with home décor to furnish the new apartment and a new clip-in hairpiece to furnish my hair. Sadly, a great deal of pulling happened over that summer. Just like freshman year, the same feelings toward my living situation and hair pulling lurked just around the corner, waiting for passing time before taking precedence in my life.

*Knock, Knock.* "Linds, I have a question on the Chemistry homework." It was Kim at my bedroom door. I had just gotten out of the shower, didn't have my bald patches covered, and had just started to blow dry my hair.

"Crap! Where is a towel? Where is a towel?" I said to myself as I frantically threw clothes from my hamper in search of the towel I had used from my shower.

"Ehm, uh, hold on one sec, Kim. I don't have any clothes on." That was a lie.

I proceeded to take my pajamas back off while also tying the towel around my head in the form of a turban. Now, I needed to find my robe to cover my body, and then I could open my bedroom door.

It became incredibly challenging to come up with reasons why I could not open my bedroom door when one of my suitemates knocked. It also seemed odd when I delayed opening the door while I rummaged for a towel to throw over my head. It was also questionable why some nights I answered my bedroom door with a towel on my head when I had not washed my hair but had already removed my hairpiece for bed.

Although I was never questioned as to my delays in answering the door, I felt ostracized from my friends due to my dissimilar situation. I would like to think that I have always been very introspective and analytical in nature, so I saw the discrepancy and distance that they could not. No matter how much my friends and family loved me, not a single one of them would be able to truly understand what my experience was like unless they lived the life of a puller. Despite being at a different developmental point in my life, I, in some ways, had more in common with the children and attendees of the *TLC* conference than my own college friends who I engaged with on a daily basis.

Aside from my parents, brothers, and previous treatment providers, no one else knew of my struggles. That was my decision. I asked my parents not to share my situation with their parents or friends, even though we are a tightly bonded family. I did not want to be judged or humiliated. I wanted to live a normal life and seen as normal; no different from non-pullers.

A common question that arises in psychology is, "What does *normal* mean?" Since I was little, I had wanted to be different. I wanted to stand out from my classmates. I wanted to be perfect when no one else was. I wanted to be the best in everything, even if no one else had the same drive. Conversely, I wanted to be seen as normal and not distinguished as having a disorder. A disorder was the antithesis of perfectionism, like oil and water, and not something I could accept for my own life. If a friend or family member had a challenge or a diagnosed disorder, I was the first person there to guide, support, and encourage, no judgment involved. However, I did not want this to be a possibility in my own life; yet, it was more than a possibility. It was my reality.

My life has been a clear example of the word *enigma*. Appropriate synonyms are words such as *mystery, puzzle, conundrum*, and *mystification*. As a little girl, I was fixated on my appearance, yet I ruined my attainment of perfection by skin picking and nail biting. In middle school, I was known as having the most gorgeous hair, yet my hair is what became my least desired feature. In college, I wanted to live an incredible, authentic, healthy lifestyle, yet I was still engaging in repetitive behaviors that were thwarting my growth process toward my full potential. I said I did not care what others thought of me, but that was far from true. I assumed that if I thought it enough, it could come true.

I still question, "What does *normal* mean?" Some individuals may think that this is the underlying goal of attending therapy. "I go to therapy because something is abnormal, and we work together to find a way to make it normal, right?" The truth is, and this isn't a novel revelation, that no one is *normal*. We all have unique oddities, faults, and quirks. Every single person on this earth is from an exclusive and exceptional genetic combination. Even twins and triplets are different from one another.

Using deductive reasoning, the only logical, coherent explanation is that *abnormal is normal*. Normal means being everything but normal. Normal is everyone who is abnormal. In my life, if I were to ever attain the level of perfection I so long desired, I would not be normal. Most likely, I would be farther from it than I am now. In sum, I have changed this definition over the years. Now, I define normal as parallel to, or synonymous with, words such as *abnormal* or *enigma*. My hope is that you keep this in mind as you continue with your life and strive for normalcy. I have, and it has helped me tremendously.

PART 4
# PATIENT TO PRACTITIONER

# 19

After the first semester of my sophomore year, I transferred from Pennsylvania to Alabama due to a change of major. I attended Auburn University for the remainder of my college education, and so did my hairpiece. I became accustomed to seeing myself with a full head of hair. The astonishment and dismay never quite dissolved when I saw my real hair, even as it was growing back.

I was unable to find a hair salon in neither Pennsylvania nor Alabama that I felt comfortable enough in exposing myself. I feared the reactions from colorists and stylists. I knew I was not the first balding client, and I knew that there were plenty of women out there in worse hair situations than mine. I also engaged in a great deal of foreshadowing which led to assumptions that there would be negative reactions from among the salon employees. The easiest thing to do was to avoid the situation. I kept my highlighted hairpiece and colored my own hair back to a generic brown, which matched the lowlights in my attachment. The piece accounted for the majority of my hair, so it was not necessary to have an exact match with my hair, only a resemblance.

Due to the cost of living in Alabama, I was able to lease a quaint, one bedroom apartment in walking distance to campus.

Having a place to call my own greatly reduced my need to create lies, excuses or sneakiness. Yet, like the issue in my one bedroom at Lehigh, the private space was endless, and Trichotillomania heightened to a new level. I continued to pull in the same settings as when I lived at home; in bed, sitting at the table doing work or studying, at the computer desk, or when talking on the phone. I never deviated from my environmental comforts or my targeted pull sites. All other sites on my body remained intact aside from my scalp. I sometimes wish that I had found satisfaction in pulling my arm and leg hair, rather than such an obvious, detrimental place. I still wonder what makes one area more sensitive than another. I have known many individuals with Trichotillomania that derive pulling pleasure from their arms and legs. I am also surprised that I was not one of those individuals given that my early years were spent targeting the skin on my arms and legs.

Thinking back over my many years of pulling, my disorder was at its peak my junior and senior year of college. Given the time that has passed to analyze and ponder, I have devised several rationales as to why this was the case at the time. First, as noted, I had my own apartment with limitless restrictions on when and where I could pull. I was in my safe space, and my motivation to stop the disorder was reduced. Second, during my pull episodes, my mind was an empty cloud of thought. I went into a trancelike state where the behavior was occurring automatically, out of awareness. I had transitioned from having identifiable thoughts to none at all, like I had mentally gone on vacation. It was as if the pull was my equivalent to lying on a beach in a remote location. Third, it had been years since attending a conference or therapy. My resources, even if only partially beneficial, were so far away from my current situation. My fourth rationale to pulling was that I had undergone a large transition from the northeast lifestyle to the southern mindset. I was removed from a place where I knew people, places, and things, and dropped in a new surrounding which I was supposed to call home. It was my decision, but it was still a critical change.

I was smart enough to recognize and admit that I needed help. I mustered up enough courage to alert my parents that my disorder had really become worse than ever.

"I really feel like I am out of control with the pulling. It is getting to the point that I am pulling whenever I am not in class or around people. I can't tie my hair up in a ponytail because I am running out of hair! There are thin areas that show through so now my only choices are to wear bandanas, hats, or my hairpiece at all times, even when I am exercising and sweating. I feel disgusting living with strands of hair everywhere all the time. I really do not know what to do."

My parents, unsurprisingly, were extremely upset but also understanding and supportive. I felt disappointed in myself and also felt upset that I had to alarm my parents, and bear bad news. My mother contacted our insurance company immediately to secure a list of providers in my area. I felt that the time had come for medication. Prior to this point, I had been resistant to entertaining the idea of prescription drugs. The possible side effects were horrifying. I had been scared off by the drug commercials on television. Who wants to get rid of anxiety but have dry mouth, night sweats, and weight gain? Hello, depression! At the time, I was uneducated and ignorant to the treatment approach, thought the worst, and hoped for the best. I was so desperate to overcome Trichotillomania that I surrendered, against my better judgment, and made an appointment with the only psychiatrist within a five-mile radius of my apartment.

The most outstanding side effects of personal concern were weight gain and difficulty with paying attention. I simply did not want to get fat, and I did not want my grades to suffer. I expressed my fears to the psychiatrist, who spoke very broken English. Dr. C was from India. She spent ample time educating me on the different types of anxiolytic drugs. An anxiolytic is a medication that reduces symptoms of anxiety. I needed one of those prescriptions just to reduce my anxious feeling about taking the drug!

Dr. C also informed me that with psychiatric medications, it was trial and error. One patient can try the first medication and feel great while a second patient can develop a host of side effects. Dosage is also a factor that requires adjustment. She said it would require time, patience, and attention to changes vastly different from how I typically felt.

We experimented with three *Selective Serotonin Reuptake Inhibitors (SSRIs)*, one *Tricyclic Antidepressant*, and one *Aminoketone Antidepressant* medication, each taken independently. I had side effects on each medication, which worked paradoxically. I pulled more because I felt unlike myself. I pulled more because I was unhappy. I pulled more because I was rapidly gaining weight and hated how I looked. I pulled more because acne was developing property and building a town on my face.

After pill jumping for one year, gaining forty pounds, and experiencing awful depression, I fired the idea of medication and felt motivated to get back on track without any aid. The consequence of my various medications created an additional barrier. Now, I was in the worst place of my life with my disorder, on top of acne, weight gain, unhappiness, and extreme fatigue.

I was in a deep, dark hole and felt hopeless, discouraged, angry at the world, and alone. It was as if I had taken a detour from my unstated goals and found myself in another country. I had many, many, circuitous miles to travel to return back to my life. There was so much damage to undo, none of which could be turned around overnight.

When someone struggling with Trichotillomania finally stops pulling, the person is reminded every single day for months or years of the damage caused. There are only long term consequences from Trichotillomania. One year free from pulling can still look like the person pulled yesterday. One year free from pulling requires the person, in some cases, to still use styling techniques, covers, and attachments. It is a constant reminder carried in our pocket even when we have overcome one of the hardest obstacles we may ever face in our life.

I was determined to use past experience, and past information gleaned from the professionals I sought, to work through the disorder. I had previously felt this sense of motivation and drive. I had this urgency before, to do it myself. This was merely a repeat of past situations.

Trichotillomania and the recovery process are both typically cyclical in nature.

I believed deep down that someday I would no longer have Trichotillomania but did not know when termination day would fall upon me. When would the disorder finally surrender? I set out on a mission to outfight it, and outsmart it. The space under my bed was a haven to my old therapy journals, monitoring charts, hypnosis CD, and folders from the *TLC* conference. I decided that was a good place to start.

One evening, towards the end of my sophomore year, I sat down to read everything in my possession. I forced myself to relive my entire experience. I forced myself to feel the feelings all over again. I forced my brain to rethink all my old thoughts and rework the process, which led to new, rational, healthy, loving thoughts. I chose to go back to my first step and retrain my feet to move, my mind to think, and my body to function. It was one night that was cleansing, exhausting, and necessary. I spent ample time reflecting on my current status in life and determining direction. I made a lot of decisions that night, including the choice to change my major, again, from Mass Communications to Psychology. I did a lot of research. I wrote in my journal, following the previous page, dated year 2000. I fell asleep listening to my former hypnotherapist, Flo, tell a hypnotic story of a forest, stairs, the color red, and a box.

# 20

I graduated from Auburn University in 2007 with a degree in psychology. On the day of college graduation, I walked across the stage with my hair attachment safely secured under my cap. When it came time to toss my cap in the air, thoughts of concern and anxiety resurfaced, just as they had in my high school graduation. While many changes transpired during my four years in college, many aspects of my life remained fixed.

My decision to pursue a degree in psychology was one that, like my decision to write this very book, elicited a host of emotions. It was a decision determined by intensive thought, which included weighing the positives and negatives. My rationale in taking the psychology path was multifaceted. I had a deep interest in the way the brain functioned, and how such functioning was translated into what we observe on a daily basis. I originally had plans to become a psychiatrist, but the countless chemistry courses required of pre-med students were not the types of pitches I could swing at. I also had a desire to help others, and make a positive impact on the world one individual at a time. I was also on a mission to find answers to Trichotillomania and *BFRB*'s from emotional, cognitive, neurological, and biological perspectives, so I could successfully treat others who were struggling.

My personal experience helped to pave the road for a new path but was not the only driving force behind my journey down that road. I saw a career as a personal decision based upon factors such as passion, curiosity, and lifelong happiness with a job. I remained confident that I would stop my hair pulling in the near future, so I never entered into the field on a hot pursuit for self-enlightenment or self-medication. I believed that my personal journey with hair pulling, nail biting, and skin picking would only enhance my abilities to be a good provider of empathy, neutrality, and unconditional positive regard because I had learned to implement these skills in my own life. I had also built a rich foundation of knowledge about *BFRB*'s due to my years of reading research studies, reading psychology journals on the topic, and conversing with experts in the field. I also felt a deep-rooted passion for my selected path. I never acknowledged that my experience with *BFRB*'s were the same as every other person who had a diagnosis of nail biting, skin picking, or hair pulling. Nonetheless, I was concerned that the perception of others on my decision would center on everything but altruism. I, therefore, kept my personal relationship with my disorders confidential.

My appetite for mental health created a craving for a whole plate of educational savories and aided in the formulation of many pertinent research questions. I also remained grounded in my recognition that experience fighting through one or two diagnosed mental health disorders was simply one or two trees within an entire forest. The field of psychology is made up of hundreds of disorders, research topics, medicines, and laws. What I possessed was a good starting point. Based upon conversation with several Auburn psychology professors, I knew that I needed to further my studies and credentials to be of use in the field. I applied to master's programs throughout the country at the start of my senior year at Auburn University.

The final year of my undergraduate career was an ongoing inner battle to overcome Trichotillomania while attempting to convince myself that I could treat other patients even if I had a problem of my own, as long as it did not interfere with my ability to be an effective clinician. I still placed a lot of pressure on myself to stop pulling my hair before I could be deemed worthy of having a position as a professional in the field. In my opinion, my credibility was determined by whether or not I was mentally healthy, not by my effectiveness as a practitioner or knowledge in the field. I am sure there are many doctors and nurses who live unsound lifestyles yet are excellent treatment providers. The validity of my opinion is not completely accurate; nonetheless, I used my viewpoint as an additional motivator in overcoming Trichotillomania.

I was very cautious not to blur the lines between the end of my experience and the beginning of my patient's experiences. Fortunately, I had some time to iron out the kinks before sitting across from my first patient. It was in one of my last psychology classes at Auburn University that I made the decision to focus my clinical and research interests on something other than Trichotillomania, to absolve any misconceptions or doubt, until my current, ongoing disorder had become something of the past.

The summer before beginning my masters program in Georgia, I worked with the eating disorder population to gain experience in something other than *BFRB*'s. This decision was commendable given the challenge of this position. In working with the population, I was able to glean a plethora of new information, expand my skill set, test my limits, and draw parallels between eating disorders and Trichotillomania. I also was assigned my first patient who had a co-morbid diagnosis of Bulimia Nervosa and Trichotillomania. I guess I was in the right place at the right time, for I never expected such an opportunity to present itself so soon. My coworkers and staff knew of my interest in Trichotillomania from a very rudimentary standpoint, so naturally I was handed the case.

It was enlightening to see hair pulling within the context of another mental health disorder. This is not uncommon. Trichotillomania is co-morbid with several other mental health disorders, including but not limited to *anxiety disorders*, *major depressive disorder*, other *impulse control disorders*, and *substance use disorders*. While I was able to gain first-hand experience and understanding of eating disorders and co-morbid disorders, I also had the opportunity to formulate my first legitimate opinion about the mental health field. Calling a disorder a *disorder* did more harm than good for the patients I saw. I had learned early on to make a conscious effort to refer to disorders as *challenges, struggles, behaviors,* or *problems.* The aforementioned terms were much more appealing and acceptable to my patients than to label a cluster of symptoms as a *disorder.* Unless I am referring to a disorder in the context of my own life, such as in this book, I am always conscious of the terminology I select. Parents and patients are generally much more receptive to *struggle* or *behavior.* The implication and the reality remain untouched, but the mental health concept is just packaged a bit more acceptably.

The transition from living on my own to living back with my parents during the summer months did not greatly alter the frequency of my pulling behavior. I continued to pull much less than I had in past years, but I still pulled enough to make Trichotillomania an ongoing struggle. It was just enough to be an annoying, pesky reminder. I continued to pull in the same settings (during more sedentary activities) and from the same area on my scalp. So much time had elapsed since I first started my behavior that I was now pulling the same hair follicles for the second or third time. I always felt concern that pulling the same hairs for the third time would be one time too many and would prevent future growth. My concern was directly linked to the thought that I may never again have a full head of my own hair.

Aside from the thought that I needed to stop immediately, I

still had difficulty with recognizing my thoughts during my pull episodes. The urgency constantly ran through my mind but there was nothing to actually break my behavioral pattern. My thoughts were not powerful or sturdy enough on their own. My emotional reaction took hold once I had stopped pulling but never during an episode. My emotions were always negative feelings toward my actions, much like a consequence.

My summer ended with complete readiness to begin the next chapter of my education at Valdosta State University in Georgia. I caravanned from Alabama to Florida to Georgia with a moving truck driven by my parents, and I was the lone scholar in tow in my vehicle. My family was in full support of my decision.

I felt anticipation and excitement for the start of graduate school, but I also mourned the loss of my trusted hairpiece that had saved me numerous occasions of embarrassment. A hairpiece thins over time when washed, dried, brushed, and flat ironed, irrespective of the initial quality. My attachment experienced all kinds of environmental conditions (i.e. rain, sweat, hail, heat, etc.), and I felt it was an appropriate time, before graduate school started, to return to the flea market. With help from my mother, I purchased a new hair attachment much like the previous one. Oddly, I then felt that much more prepared for my master's program to commence.

I had not stepped foot in the flea market since my first visit to the hair stand. I was flooded with emotion as I reminisced on my initial experience. In comparison, I was not nervous or apprehensive. I had come to the realization that life would have been more difficult had I not risked the embarrassment I felt the first time I stood in front of the hair booth. I selected a new attachment similar to my last, and a thought crossed my mind. "I hope this one is as good as the one before, because I am going to need it to last me a while. There is a lot of hair growth that needs to take place. I wish for my own hair to grow back and for graduate school to be an amazing experience." I have learned that positive thinking increases the propensity for positive results.

# 21

I sat in my very first psychology graduate class, and that is when reality struck me hard, like a punch to the stomach. I was overwhelmed by the litany of novel terminology as well as an unsettling, panicky feeling in my gut. It was the same foreign feeling I endured when I sat across the room from my first patient with Trichotillomania and Bulimia Nervosa at the inpatient center that summer. The foreign feeling was one of hypocrisy. I was a complete liar, a total fraud, a scam artist, a trickster! What was I doing? I was putting myself in the position to help others with the exact thing I suffered from on a daily basis. I felt like I was lying to everyone in my graduate program. I actually lied when asked why I had an interest in pursuing a career in psychology. The question was asked in every class the first day of my first semester. I continued to put on a poker face and make up a lame excuse; lame albeit believable.

"I am fascinated by the way people think." While this was true, this was not the complete truth.

I lied to every professor and every classmate. I poured so much energy into concealing a lifelong problem. I was in school to learn to be an expert in providing treatment to those in need, when I was in dire need of care myself. I desperately wanted to believe I was getting better just because I was taking the appropriate steps to advance myself as a professional. In reality, I lacked credibility. I had not found the solution to my own problem but was setting myself up to sit across from parents in a therapy room and claim that I could be of service. In my opinion, I was a walking contradiction...a hypocrite.

In addition to tricking my professors and myself, I was a trickster to my parents. I told them I had stopped pulling because it sounded amazing and felt liberating to vocalize, even if it was far from the truth. I was hoping that if I acted like I was *healed* and *normal*, and put myself through the motions, that possibly - hopefully - maybe - it would miraculously come true.

Each evening when I left campus, I felt more like a phony. The more information I learned the more I questioned my reality and the direction of my life. I felt as though I had backed myself into a corner and then fallen down a deep hole, which I had personally dug. My same thoughts on the topic played to a nauseating degree:

> • *Eventually I am going to be paid to do a job that I am lying about.*
>
> • *What am I going to do when I graduate in two years but am still struggling with Trichotillomania?*
>
> • *Now that my parents think I have stopped pulling, they are likely feeling so hopeful, relieved, and happy. I cannot let them down.*

*• How long am I going to do this? When do I finally get a grip on life?*

*• When do I grow up and start acting responsibly toward my own body?*

*• My professors are so impressed by how much I know about therapy, research, and disorders. If they only knew why, I would probably be excused from the program.*

Each week I pondered how to create an escape for myself from the program. On the one hand, I appreciated my professors and enjoyed what I was learning. I excelled in the classroom and it was rewarding to be a star student in my cohort. I thrived on working hard and reaping benefits. I learned from my classmates. I felt like I was part of something special and unique. Conversely, the longer I remained in my program, the harder it would be to excuse myself, due to time and money investments, and the more I felt like a bad person.

I weighed the pros and cons of telling my professors about my struggle with Trichotillomania. They would all surely understand, for they are psychologists and their job is to be nonjudgmental, right? Perhaps they would want to interview me and pick my brain about what I knew about *BFRB*'s. That would be cool. Further, it would be amazing to be able to create a presentation with a *Q&A* to offer to all the students in the master's program. At the same time, there is the chance that I would be told that I need too much personal therapy to be useful to anyone else. Maybe the head of the program would ask me to take a leave of absence until my disorder was resolved, which could be a rather lengthy amount of time. I could never face the humiliation of such a request. Being truthful was not an option. I had become the true definition of the word *trichster* in more than one way. Nothing about who I was at that point in my life was appealing or truthful.

I first heard of the term *trichster* at the *TLC* conference. A *trichster* is someone who has been diagnosed with Trichotillomania. I met that definition. I was also a *trickster* because no one knew of my hair problems. Each time I accepted a compliment with a thank you, I was actually welcoming a lie with open arms. I was taking hold of an accolade I did not deserve to have, yet never verbalized my dismay. My visual appearance was a lie. I focused attention on appearing perfect, while each subsequent pull episode floated me farther and farther from perfection and long-term career goals. Each pull-free day inched me closer to the life I desired. The endless back and forth was relentless and exhausting, and frankly just not good enough. Essentially, self-sabotage was my modus operandi. I had the chance to do anything I wanted to do, to be whomever I wanted to be, and to look however I wanted to look. The only thing stopping me from reaching my potential was my own behavior.

I found myself in a place where I did not want

Trichotillomania, and the surrounding self-sabotaging ideals, to be the paradigm for my life. However, *wanting* and *doing* are two very different concepts. Motivation is confusing in that sense. I define motivation as the underlying force that drives a behavior. The behavior itself can be something either positive or negative. However, motivation is not behavior. If a person is motivated to do something, it may sound like a great idea, but it does not imply that anything is actually changing. Motivation does not equate to productivity. Depending on the level of motivation, *wanting* and *doing* can be vastly distant. At what level does motivation need to reach to elicit behavioral change?

There were many times in my life where my level of motivation to stop hair pulling elevated. Each peak was always a result of an external factor, such as the recognition of time and effort put towards extensive therapy, or the *TLC* conference, for example. This is referred to as extrinsic motivation. As humans, we have the ability to be propelled by both extrinsic and intrinsic motivation.

As it relates to Trichotillomania, none of my extrinsic motivators were enduring. This leads me to answer the following questions. What type of motivation do I need in order to experience change? To what extent do I need to feel motivation in order to bring permanent behavioral change to my life? Neither of these questions is unusual, for we likely think about these concepts often, just in a different context. Motivation is subjective and is felt differently from person to person.

How much physical anguish does a female need to experience before she actually leaves the abusive relationship? To what level does a gentleman with a drinking problem need to reach before he surrenders his behavior? How many more pounds will a diabetic with hypercholesterolemia gain before following a diet regimen with fidelity? We can all relate in one way or another.

I spent a considerable amount of time reflecting on the ebb and flow of my disorder and my parallel sources of motivation. Personally, up until my first semester of graduate school, the negative consequences of my behaviors had not culminated into something grand enough to make the pulling no longer worth it. I needed to reach the point where I did not see and feel the benefit of pulling. I had exerted so much mental energy and attention to the lies and aesthetic coverings that, although I was miserable and suffered, my disorder was manageable.

The years of time and effort spent on styling my hair, on therapy, on medication failures, on side effects, on disappointing my parents, on lying, on hypnosis, on physical changes, on humiliation, on embarrassment, and on entrapment were somehow not enough extrinsic motivation. I needed to feel something rooted deep inside me to drive me to hate my hair pulling behavior. I tend to think that the consequences of my disorder were tolerable because they all did not occur simultaneously every day. Instead, a sole consequence was easier to dismiss. In reflecting on how devastating the disorder was for so many years, I wish I could have experienced a strong enough reason early on, but it was just a delayed process, which was largely a product of time.

# 22

It was in 2008, toward the end of my second semester of graduate school, when I became worn down. I was exhausted. The repetitive nature of my *BFRB* as well as the ruminating negative thoughts of my life as a *trichster* finally got the best of me. I always viewed my disorder as a boxing match. I, the bad ass, stood in the red corner (with a matching red bandana on my head) while the Trichotillomania ogre paced in the blue corner. I always envisioned that one day the ogre, to indicate surrender, would throw the towel down. The end did not happen that way at all. Instead, I was the one to surrender.

I assume that many of you decided to read this book to learn about *BFRB*'s out of curiosity and with the intention of getting answers to possibly the two most important questions to come from this topic. "Did I eventually stop? How did I do it?" I feel such immense pleasure and happiness, more than any episode of hair pulling ever offered, to share the news that I did stop pulling my hair. I so badly wanted to live a genuine, authentic life where I could be true to myself and truthful with every individual in my life. I wanted to be successful, healthy, and happy. I wanted to make a difference. I wanted to make my family proud of the life I chose to live. None of my goals allowed for room for a time-consuming, threatening, disheartening, ugly ogre of a disorder.

When I chose to surrender, I won.

After class one night, I was sitting in my room and I started thinking about the one *TLC* conference I had attended years ago with my parents. I found the pile of notes from the conference under my bed, the same place I had kept my important information in my Auburn apartment. The conference experience had such an impact, was so educational, and so moving. It did not take much time or thought to decide on registering for that year's *TLC* conference. I attended the first one as a patient. I wanted to attend this one as a mental health practitioner for the purposes of gaining new information on research and treatment. I registered for the weekend and immediately provided ample notice to my professors for the one class day I would miss due to traveling to Boston.

A month later, I was sitting at Tallahassee airport awaiting the start of boarding. I felt excited and energized at the thought of making so many professional connections and learning of the latest research. My professors were very supportive of my desire to attend the conference and asked that I share what I learned, upon returning to Georgia. It was a different experience traveling to a professional conference as a semi-professional without family, friends, coworkers, or classmates. In the back of my mind, I continued to remind myself that I was still a patient too. Although it had been years since I had been to therapy for my own purposes, I knew that I needed to take the time to attend some of the seminars, which targeted individuals struggling with Trichotillomania.

The conference was held at a large hotel convention center, which smoothed the travel process. It was nice to be in the same building as where I was staying without having to brave the inclement weather, rent a car, or follow driving directions. Although I felt excited and energized, my fictitious identity also accompanied me to Boston, which kept me feeling a bit uneasy. I felt nervous that the lead researchers and practitioners would question my attendance at both the professional and patient seminars, for everyone else was identified as either a professional provider or patient/patient's family. I hoped that with the number of attendees, I would fall unnoticed among the crowd.

I checked into my room, which was rather peaceful and spacious. I hung up my dress pants in the hotel room, and lined up my high heels on the floor. I had packed business casual attire as I wanted to look presentable when interacting with the other treatment providers and researchers. I freshened up at the vanity, hung my nametag around my neck, and ventured out to the welcome session.

My initial glance around the conference took me right back to the conference I attended with my parents years ago. I found it so interesting that although years had passed and the understanding of the disorder had advanced, the vision of what a *TLC* conference looked like had been left untouched. I was sitting at a large circular table next to and across from men and women with bald heads or wigs. Like my first experience, it took my eyes some time to adjust to what it was like seeing so many people without hair, eyebrows, and eyelashes all in the same room. I felt just as overwhelmed as the first time my eyes focused on such a sight. I noticed there were even more children without eyebrows and eyelashes in attendance than the first conference. I felt deep sadness, yet also felt hopeful that their parents had introduced them to a weekend experience where they could be natural, open, and accepted with or without hair.

Shortly after the welcome session, we were instructed to break away to the first official information session we had individually selected from the list of choices. I had prearranged my schedule to accommodate for an equal balance of professional and personal seminars. Many of the seminars had the same presenters and the same topics as years prior; yet, the material discussed had advanced with time. I took notes and asked engaging questions. I also started to formulate potential research project ideas from some of the points presented. After just one seminar, I felt grateful for my decision to attend my second conference.

Each day, either lunch or dinner was served in the large banquet hall. The first night, attendees were free to explore away from the hotel for dinner and evening activities. I felt very exhausted from the travel, emotional energy of the conference, and influx of information. My private hotel room, equipped with movies and room service, sounded much more enticing than layering clothes and fighting through the harsh winter winds. I ordered food and reviewed my notes from the day while awaiting dinner's arrival. I also planned to go to sleep early as the morning session began around 8:00 am. I had been through *conference mode* before and remembered that the second day, which was the first full day, was tiring, long, and arduous.

The second day of the conference something unexpected and life changing occurred. After the morning session, which everyone conjointly attended, I stood from the random table with which I sat in anticipation of finding the first session of the day. As I turned around, I spotted an incredibly attractive lady sitting with a handsome man. She had the most beautiful hair I had ever seen, and he was bald. Amongst a room of individuals either without hair, or with wigs, anyone with their own, natural hair does not go unnoticed. This lady not only had what looked to be her own hair, but she had a lot of it, and it was gorgeous. I thought that it was so nice that she was there to support her husband or boyfriend. At that moment, I hoped that I would someday have a partner that would be as supportive as she was to her significant other. I also hoped that my *someday-supportive partner* would not be supporting me at a hair pulling conference. Hopefully, I would be well past Trichotillomania by then!

I was feeling rather outgoing and confident, so I approached the couple, who were still sitting at their table. The lady was so pretty that I assumed she would probably be a bit inhospitable. In addition to making an incorrect assumption, I made another big mistake once she made eye contact with me.

"Hi, I'm Lindsey. I saw you both from across the room and your gorgeous hair caught my attention. You are so lucky to have such beautiful hair. I love the highlights. Great color. So, are you here to learn more about Trich and support your boyfriend? Is this your first conference?"

I saw she was not wearing a wedding ring, but they were holding hands, so I knew it had to be her boyfriend. That was not the mistake I was referencing.

"Aw, you are so sweet. I am Stephanie and this is Cory, my boyfriend. This is our first conference, and I am really exhausted. It is all so overwhelming. All this information and all these people everywhere makes me want to take a nap. (Laughs.) That's funny you think Cory is the one with Trichotillomania. No, he just shaves his head because he likes how it looks. I'm actually the one that pulls. Cory is here to support me. He is the best."

Wait, what? Did I hear her correctly? How could she possibly struggle with Trichotillomania with hair like that? I learned from this interaction, and would never again assume that I can differentiate patients from support systems. Now, I always ask.

"Wow, I would have never known. Your hair is gorgeous. Do you have extensions or a piece, if you do not mind me asking?"

"Yes, I have a piece, see? It's attached at the top, which is why I usually wear my hair like this, parted *half-up half-down*. I only pull from one small area on my scalp, but my problem area is my eyebrows. I haven't had any real eyebrows for years. I draw them on every morning. I also pulled my eyelashes for a long time, but that has gotten better."

I was amazed how open and honest she was. It was refreshing to finally have a conversation with someone else struggling with Trichotillomania, who was beautiful, sweet, and stylish. I had never met anyone prior to Stephanie whom I felt could really relate to me. We had an immediate connection. Stephanie, Cory, and I decided to compare schedules and attend several of the seminars together. I had never felt so close to someone so quickly. She became an instant friend, and I felt like Cory was there to support me as well. I explained to them that I was at the conference as a patient and future practitioner. They were so impressed that I had chosen a career path, which would allow me to treat others like Stephanie and me.

The more we conversed, the more we were shocked. We had so many things in common. We were perfectionists. We were overachievers. She was a few years my elder and therefore had just obtained her master's degree in occupational therapy. We both came from strong, loving, supportive families. We both got overwhelmed and stressed easily when there was a lot going on in the environment at the same time. We both fatigued easily, and we both happened to share in some of the same digestive issues. One thing that she mentioned, which resonated with me, was that she had an addiction to carbohydrates and sugar. I did too, but I never told anyone about it.

My sugar and carbohydrate addiction was something I later recognized as being a negative influence on my hair pulling. The more carbohydrates and sugar I consumed, the more I would pull my hair afterward. I also felt an immense lack of control around carbohydrates to the point where I had to stop buying breads and sweets altogether because I was unable to have just a taste. I would either not buy anything or binge on a whole loaf of bread in one day. Separately, Stephanie told me of her addiction with sugar and desserts. We both struggled with the same sugar binges followed by the feeling of incredible bloat, abdominal distention, and sickness. Then we would pull later that night. It was odd that we shared this pattern.

Based upon my analysis of my addiction to bread, pasta, bagels, and dried fruit (although sounding healthy, dried fruit is loaded with sugar and especially harmful when I ate close to one pound daily), I later educated myself on the detrimental nature of sugar and carbohydrates to my organs, blood sugar, and brain functioning.

I successfully eliminated the food *drug;* and have remained consciously aware of what I ingest. I now know that my years of high sugar intake played a part in my pulling urges. Yet, I never came across any research which tested this connection, or which stated that high sugar or high carbohydrate consumption caused pulling urges. This was solely a connection that I found to be true in my own life. Stephanie found this to hold true in her life, as well. Nonetheless, it was incredibly challenging to break my cravings, but I knew I needed to.

By the end of the conference, I left with a new notebook full of information, a folder of handouts and diagrams, an enlivened desire to pursue my degree in psychology, a newfound motivation to cease my behavior, and a new best friend who felt like the sister I never had. Stephanie and I exchanged information and agreed that we would communicate every few days and serve as accountability partners to counteract the disorder. Unfortunately, I lived in Georgia at the time while she lived in New York City. Cory lived in Boston. I knew I would see them again and also felt confident that she would remain in my life forever.

It is miraculous what the commonalities of a disorder will do to bring together two individuals. I had never met a person who had experienced and felt the same things as I did. If you are struggling with the disorder, or are a parent of a child with Trichotillomania, I encourage you to seek out a like-minded individual with similar experiences who can provide a space for reciprocal interaction and understanding. There is something so powerful about being able to confide in someone that has not exactly, but very closely, lived through what you have also experienced.

Stephanie became as good as, or better than, any therapist I ever had. Unlike a therapist, who is also highly recommended, Stephanie was not able to provide professional treatment interventions but was able to provide the closest form of empathy and reflection that I will likely ever experience. Although her pulling presented differently at the time of the conference as far as severity and manifestation of body sites, I was able to totally relate to what she was doing to herself, for I was in that place at one point in my life.

# 23

The moment I returned to Georgia, I felt like I arrived equipped with a secret that no one else in the state possessed. I felt like my self-esteem had grown in just one weekend's time. I suddenly viewed myself as so much better than my struggles. I remember the day I stopped pulling. It all came to an end. How did I do it? I became tired.

I did not beat Trichotillomania. It's not like I was introduced to something I had not previously tried. There wasn't a new medication introduced to the market. If only it were that easy. I did not stop as a result of a certain therapeutic skill or intervention, although it all helped carry me to a better place. Ultimately, I stopped because I became exhausted. You know the boxing match I mentioned where I stood in the red corner and Trichotillomania stood in the blue corner? Well, the fight was not meant to last a lifetime. I knew it would eventually cease, for a professional boxer had not trained me, nor had I conditioned for long-lasting endurance. I did not beat Trichotillomania, and it did not beat me, either.

The day I returned from my second conference, I came to my own realization that I did not have to win or lose the fight. I could simply stop fighting all together. I could walk away without any major repercussions beyond some scalp damage, and that sounded so much better than continuing to fight. I took my hands down from my head and walked away with as much grace and dignity as I could muster.

I gave up. I walked away. I pulled so much hair from my scalp for so long that I literally got sick of it and just stopped. The desire to pull dissipated. I did not want to pull out my hair anymore, so I didn't. My urges subsided and never really revisited me. In 2008, the day I returned from the conference in Boston, was the last time I ever pulled my hair. For the duration of my life, I had taken the approach that I wanted to be the best in everything, and that I would never quit. In the context of my disorder, however, I became a quitter. Currently, I am a deplorable facilitator of pulling, more like a pathetic definition of a patient. This may be the first time in which I am proud to announce that I am lacking motivation to complete a task, and that I am awful at an activity. For the first time, my poor motivation, imperfection, and failure resulted in overwhelming euphoria and great reward.

I graduated with my master's degree in Clinical/Counseling Psychology in 2009 and started a doctoral program at The University of Iowa ten days later. I wanted to see how much more I could learn about Trichotillomania and assumed that a doctoral education would provide that opportunity. Shortly after beginning my doctorate, I came to the realization that my informal education, called life, was beyond sufficient. I was able to develop specialized training and obtain experience in a plethora of mental health treatment settings while attending my doctorate program; yet, I found that I was essentially teaching my professors and classmates more about *BFRB*'s than they could teach me. This situation was not necessarily negative as I was able to hone in on research and presentation skills. Further, I was provided an enriching, supportive environment where I was challenged in other ways.

I generated many research questions and formulated several sound hypotheses during my doctoral program. However, I didn't have interest in dedicating my life to either research or academia and became overly eager to work in the field with patients struggling much as I had. Now that the hair-pulling hurdle was cleared, I was able to treat patients competently, tactfully, and truthfully; I felt that I was ready for my career.

My hairpieces played a pivotal role in my life for many years. Although I stopped pulling my hair toward the middle of 2008, the results of my disorder far outlasted my repetitive behavior. As I mentioned earlier on, this is an unfortunate aspect of the disorder. It is challenging to live life after overcoming such a difficulty while still having to face the daily reminder of what I did to myself. There is no one else to blame, but I grew to understand that blame never helped the situation. Therefore, I withheld all blame and judgment and just let my hair grow on its own time.

I was in the middle of a snowstorm in Iowa City in February of 2010. The weather channel reported negative twelve degrees Fahrenheit, and the city shut down due to another winter blizzard. I stepped out of a scalding hot shower after washing my hair and stared at my clip-in hairpiece lying on the bathroom counter. The weathered hairpiece that was once voluminous and luscious looked tired, thin, and limp, much like I had felt toward my ongoing struggle with Trichotillomania that day back in 2008. I dried my hair in the same fashion I had for many years, and climbed into bed without my hairpiece. The piece was attached with metal clips, which irritated my scalp if my head rested on a pillow. I left it on the counter in the bathroom when I went to bed that night, just like every other evening.

I woke up the following morning and went into my bathroom to wash and dress for an exciting day of being snowed-in. Once my contacts were inserted, my makeup was applied, and I was dressed, I returned back to the bathroom mirror. I intended to attach my hairpiece as I had every morning for the past ten years. The crown portion of my head had grown in thicker than before I started pulling. My hair looked fluffy and full as compared to my hairpiece, which was still lying on the bathroom counter. I ran my fingers through my hair and then walked to my kitchen.

I returned to my bathroom and elevated the lights to their maximum setting. I secured my hair, of various lengths, back in a ponytail. I started crying tears of deep-felt joy as I took the kitchen scissors and cut my entire ponytail off. I did not discuss this with anyone, including Stephanie. I hadn't planned on doing what I did. I spent years hoping and waiting the day would come where I would be able to live a life with a full head of hair and free from hairspray, gel, clips, and attachments. It is a trichster's dream!

That morning, upon looking in the mirror, was the precise moment that I realized I would be okay walking out of my house with just my own hair. I wanted to have the honor of giving myself the best haircut I could ever have, a gift to myself, despite what it actually looked like.

It was impulsive, and it was the most liberating thing I have ever experienced. I imagine streaking is sort of like what I did. Fun. Exhilarating. Exciting. Liberating. A natural high. A rush. I had never cut anyone's hair before that day. It may have looked better if my tears hadn't blurred my vision. I must admit I did an amazing job under the circumstance. I did not call my parents to tell them what I did. I knew that a picture sent by text message was the best way to deliver such good news. I continued crying tears of happiness as I sent the picture; a type of happiness that no other life event would likely ever afford me.

I still have all of my previous hairpieces in a box in the closet at my parent's house. They are thinned, tattered, and nappy. At one point I considered throwing them away, but I can't. My hair attachments represent monumental years of my life when I chose to conceal who I really was.

It was February 16, 2010 when I gave myself my first and last haircut. Coincidentally, that was the three-year anniversary of the very day Britney Spears had her famous, humiliating, public meltdown and shaved her head. While she and I had completely different motives for our respective haircuts, and while I have never met the celebrity, I know there is one fact to which Britney Spears and I would both agree. *Life is Trichy.*

# Afterword

After completing a total of nine years of college and earning several degrees, I entered into the field of psychology to practice what I learned. I worked in various settings with a range of populations and ages, but in the end found my most intriguing and rewarding work to stem from body focused repetitive behaviors. Currently, I see patients with the aforementioned struggles in a private practice setting.

Despite the years that have passed since I last fought with Trichotillomania, I still wear a hairpiece, as a result of years of pulling, and my hair grows very, very slowly. My hair will eventually get there, but it takes time, and I was too impatient in wanting long hair again. After I had given myself the short haircut that chilly day in Iowa, I never thought the look of my own short hair was as becoming as long hair. Only a few months passed before I ordered a new hairpiece, so I wouldn't have to spend years waiting for my hair to grow out.

While I have gone on to help and treat many children, adolescents, and adults diagnosed with Trichotillomania, I keep in mind that I am still in recovery. I continue my awareness of current habits and lifestyle patterns. I remain actively engaged in taking the right steps to keep my life balanced and healthy. I recognize I need much more sleep than the average adult, so I prioritize and manage my time to allow for such. I do not know if my need for sleep has anything to do with the problems I had, nor have I found any research on this. Perhaps, getting enough sleep is something that helps keep urges away.

Also included in my implemented lifestyle changes, is the conscious decision to keep my sugar intake to a minimum. I take a daily multivitamin and replace most fruits with vegetables in order to maintain balanced nutrition. I have found that sugar is like a drug to my body. The taste of a little drop is a tease as opposed to satiating. If I have a little, I will have a lot. The simple solution for this situation is to tell myself that I will only have a few small bites and walk away. That never happens. I recognize my weaknesses, and I know my limitations. I know how my mind and body function, and while it is within my ability to change my thoughts and actions, it is easier for me to remain motivated in implementing something that has multifarious health benefits. Why should I work so hard to try to find a balance of sugar in my life when I really do not need it at all? Ultimately, the less I consume, the healthier I can potentially live and feel. This is something I have found works for me and keeps the pulling urges far, far away. However, what works for me may not work for you. If only it was *that* clear-cut. There isn't a mathematical equation to solve the hair-pulling problem.

Along with sleep and the proper nutrition, I engage in light exercise a few times a week. I find that extreme exercise, for me, causes more fatigue than benefit. I try to do activities that I find pleasurable rather than exhausting: yoga, walking, bike riding, and dancing. I believe that the proper level of stimulation is beneficial to keeping physically and mentally healthy.

In addition to working with patients and discussing the various *BFRB's* with parents, I find time to communicate with Stephanie regularly. We continue to learn more about each other on a weekly basis and continue to be amazed. We are now at very different places in our lives, and our schedules (along with being in different time zones) do not always work to our advantage. Nonetheless, we have past experiences that keep our connection strong and indefinite. When I told Stephanie I had decided to write a book, she supported me and felt excited for the opportunity to get our story out to the public. Public awareness of *BFRB*'s is imperative for the advancement of funding and for better understanding of the disorders.

In order to find an appropriate editor and cover designer for my project, I spent a great deal of time communicating and networking. Naturally, an initial query led to offering a brief synopsis of my manuscript to aid potential editors in determining their level of interest. Of the twenty-something proposals received, I was unbelievably surprised and moved by how many responses included interest and personal information regarding someone who knew someone with a *BFRB*. All it took from me was the generation and mailing of twenty-something emails to obtain connections to many people who could relate to my situation, and project. I hope this information is encouraging to those of you who fear telling someone about your struggles and behaviors. I regret not being more open sooner, for it likely would have prevented a lot of endured guilt, shame, and deceitfulness.

I feel an overwhelming sense of accomplishment for having braved my fears in sharing my story. At the same time I feel incredibly saddened, as if the end of the book is representational of the end of a large part of my life. This is not incredibly true given that I will continue to be in the psychology field for many years with hopes of interacting with many other individuals with Trichotillomania. I also feel nervous about publication. My story will be revealed to all my family members, closest friends, professors, past relationships, and anyone else whom I may have had meaningful interactions with. I apologize to everyone that I lied to in attempts to keep my disorder hidden.

I believe that I experienced my struggles for a reason. My hope is that I will be an example of courage and confidence to all the individuals, family and friends included, who are struggling with their place in life, their self-perception, and their motivation to make positive life changes to achieve full potential, irrespective of whether or not Trichotillomania is present.

I sat in a local, hip, coffee shop in Los Angeles, California while undergoing my final edit in the summer of 2014. Sitting directly across from me was a good-looking man in his late twenties or early thirties. While typing away on his laptop, I couldn't help but notice both his keyboard and his hair occupied his hands. He kept shamelessly, unconsciously twirling and pulling at the front portion of his light brown hair. How ironic. The timing of this encounter could not have been any more convenient. I interpreted what I saw as a sign that the book project, which had been my focus for the last few months, would be well received, useful, and necessary. It was as if he had been strategically placed in front of me. I wondered if he was aware of what he was doing. I wondered if he had ever heard of Trichotillomania. I made a new friend that day in the Los Angeles coffee house…

# Resources

I know how difficult it has been for my parents to find information over the years on research, treatment, and answers to Trichotillomania and Body Focused Repetitive Behaviors. Further, information is always changing as new therapists and doctors open practices, and salons come and go. I started compiling a list of resources including websites, hair salons, practitioners, etc., yet came to realize that I continued to modify the list over and over again as time passed. However, I certainly did not want to close this book without leaving my readers with information to take home.

## Hair Salons

The few hair salons I have been to that specialized in hair replacement, alopecia, and Trichotillomania were found through scouring the web using the aforementioned as key words. I would hope that there is a salon in every area where one is sought. My recommendation is to search online, or check your local city magazines. Another option is to contact Hair Club (www.hairclub.com) with the intent of being directed to a salon that does have specialization in this. Also, always ask to see if private rooms are available. One of my worst experiences was the first time I decided to visit a salon that had never seen a patchy scalp nor heard of Trichotillomania. I felt humiliated, embarrassed, and dehumanized. All of the stylists and colorists were sequentially called over to look at my hair. I wish I could say I was exaggerating. I put on a brave face for all of the salon staff to see, but as soon as they were finished gathering around to look at my hair and rinsing the color, I ran out. I got into my mother's car and started crying hysterically. Unfortunately, she had to go in and pay.

Following my unnerving salon experience, there was a one year period where I refused to step foot into a salon. Instead, I colored my own hair which never looked as good, but I had to accept it for the time being. Visiting a salon is something that women and men typically view as pampering and relaxing; yet, only one who has struggled with Trichotillomania would know that this is like a death sentence. I avoided it at all costs or delayed any hair improvements for weeks or even months. A visit to a salon that is not experienced in servicing clients with Trichotillomania can be traumatic.

## Support Groups, Therapy and Research

With the popularity of websites, blogs, online forums, and social media platforms, it seems as though there is something for everyone on the internet. Nonetheless, quantity should not be mistaken for quality. Of the various websites I have stumbled upon or interacted with, my default website is www.trich.org. This is the website for the Trichotillomania Learning Center which I previously discussed. This website provides invaluable information for local support groups, practitioners, and current research studies in each state. At this website, you will also find research articles and resources for individuals, parents, and children/teenagers. If you are not visiting a therapist and support group regularly, I highly encourage you to do so. It takes an incredibly strong individual to recognize and admit that a problem exists and then elicit help from an outside source. It took me some time to come to accept that visiting a therapist was not a sign of weakness or failure but an opportunity to better myself by building a new skill set or strengthening the one I currently had. Further, there is great healing value in being part of a group, which is larger than you.

Attending a support group or group therapy has been scientifically proven to be advantageous. Irvin Yalom is an existential psychiatrist and psychotherapist, celebrated for his identification of curative factors associated with group therapy, of which support groups are a part. Although not an exhaustive list, group therapy provides instillation of hope, a sense of belonging, and universality, i.e. recognition of a common problem that provides a common bond for group members.

From a networking standpoint, a large challenge in the area of Trichotillomania is finding people like you (for those reading who struggle with the disorder or know someone that is). This is due to the shame and humiliation of the disorder

and the immense desire on the part of the parent or individual
to keep the topic buried. Yes, this prevents embarrassment,
but the privacy creates consequences on various levels. Why
do we commonly hear about Autism or Obsessive Compulsive
Disorder? It is not necessarily that these disorders, in reality,
are more prevalent among the population but rather discussed
because they are known. The unknown cannot be discussed,
learned, or researched. Exposure to Trichotillomania creates
opportunities to educate our country and solicit funding for
continued research in the field.

## Associations and Sources of Information

This is not an exhaustive list. I encourage you to also seek out
local organizations and resources. Many states have their own
mental health organizations and upon researching, you may
be surprised to find an association for Obsessive Compulsive
Disorder or Anxiety Disorders specific to your state. For
example, I know of *OCD New Jersey*, an affiliate of the
*International OCD Foundation.*

American Psychological Association
750 First Street, NE
Washington, DC 20002-4242
800-374-2721 phone
www.apa.org

Anxiety and Depression Association of America

8701 Georgia Ave., Suite 412
Silver Spring, MD 20910
240-485-1001 phone
240-485-1035 fax
www.adaa.org

International OCD Foundation, Inc.
18 Tremont Street, Suite 903
Boston, MA 02108
617-973-5801 phone
617-973-5803 fax
info@iocdf.org
www.ocfoundation.org

National Alliance on Mental Illness
3803 N. Fairfax Dr., Suite 100
Arlington, VA 22203
703-524-7600 phone
703-524-9094 fax
www.nami.org

National Institute of Mental Health
Science Writing, Press, and Dissemination Branch
6001 Executive Boulevard, Room 6200, MSC 9663
Bethesda, MD 20892-9663
866-615-6464 toll-free phone
 301-443-4279 fax
nimhinfo@nih.gov
www.nimh.nih.gov

Trichotillomania Learning Center, Inc.
207 McPherson Street, Suite H
Santa Cruz, CA 95060-5863
831-457-1004 phone
831-427-5541 fax

info@trich.org
www.trich.org

## Books for patients and parents on BFRB's

None of the following books are a replacement for therapy, but rather used as a supplement. This is not an exhaustive list but merely the books with which I have familiarity. Further, make sure you do your own research. Ask who the authors are and what their credentials are in writing a psychology help book.

*A Parent Guide to Hair Pulling Disorder: Effective Parenting Strategies for Children with Trichotillomania*
Suzanne Mouton-Odom and Ruth Goldfinger Golomb, 2013

*Doesn't It Hurt?: Confessions of Compulsive Hair Pullers*
Sandy Rosenblatt, 2014

*Help for Hair Pullers: Understanding and Coping with Trichotillomania*
Nancy Keuthen, 2001

*Pearls: Meditations on Recovery from Hair Pulling and Skin Picking*
Christina Pearson, 2010

*Skin Picking: The Freedom to Finally Stop*
Annette Pasternak and Tammy Fletcher, 2014

*The Hair Pulling "Habit" and You: How to Solve the Trichotillomania Puzzle, Revised Edition*
Ruth Goldfinger Golomb and Sherrie Mansfield Vavrichek, 2000

*The Hair-Pulling Problem: A Complete Guide to Trichotillomania*
Fred Penzel, 2003


*Trichotillomania, Skin Picking, and Other Body-Focused Repetitive
Behaviors*
Jon Grant, Dan Stein, Douglas Woods, and Nancy Keuthen, 2011


*Urges: Hope and Inspiration for People with Trichotillomania and
Other Mysterious Compulsions*
Gary Hennerberg, 2009


*What to Do When Bad Habits Take Hold: A Kid's Guide to
Overcoming Nail Biting and More*
Dawn Huebner, 2008


*What's Happening To My Child? A Guide for Parents of Hair Pullers*
Cheryn Salazar, 2011


## Books for practitioners on treating BFRB's

*Clinical Guide to Obsessive Compulsive and Related Disorders*
Jon Grant, Samuel Chamberlain, and Brian Odlaug, 2014


*Obsessive-Compulsive Disorder and Its Spectrum: A Life Span
Approach*
Eric Storch and Dean McKay, 2014


*Psychological Treatment of Obsessive-Compulsive Disorder:
Fundamentals and Beyond*
Martin Antony, Christine Purdon, and Laura Summerfeldt, 2007


*Tic Disorder, Trichotillomania, and Other Repetitive Behavior*

*Disorders: Behavioral Approaches to Analysis and Treatment*
Douglas Woods and Raymond Miltenberger, 2006

*Treating Trichotillomania: Cognitive-Behavioral Therapy for Hair Pulling and Related Problems (Series in Anxiety and Related Disorders)*
Martin Franklin and David Tolin, 2010

*Trichotillomania: An ACT-enhanced Behavior Therapy Approach Therapist Guide (Treatments That Work)*
Douglas Woods and Michael Twohig, 2008

*Trichotillomania: An ACT-enhanced Behavior Therapy Approach Workbook (Treatments That Work)*
DouglasWoods and Michael Twohig, 2008

*Trichotillomania, Skin Picking, and Other Body-Focused Repetitive Behaviors*
Jon Grant, Dan Stein, Douglas Woods, and Nancy Keuthen, 2011

# References

Jean Piaget. *Play, Dreams, and Imitation in Childhood.* (W. W. Norton and Company, Inc., 1962).

David Elkind. *Child Development and Education: A Piagetian Perspective.* (Oxford University Press, 1976).

B.F. Skinner. *About Behaviorism.* (Vintage, 1976).

American Psychiatric Association. *Diagnostic and Statistical Manual of Mental Disorders, 5th ed. (DSM-5).* (American Psychiatric Publishing, Incorporated, 2013).

American Psychiatric Association. *Diagnostic and Statistical Manual of Mental Disorders, Text Revision, 4th ed. (DSM-IV-TR).* (American Psychiatric Publishing, Incorporated, 2000).

Woods, D. W. & Twohig, M. P. *Treatments that work: Trichotillomania-An ACT-enhanced behavior therapy approach therapist guide.* (Oxford University Press, 2008).

American Psychiatric Association. *Diagnostic and Statistical Manual of Mental Disorders, Text Revision, 4th ed. (DSM-IV-TR).* (American Psychiatric Publishing, Incorporated, 2000).

Tolin, D. F., Franklin, M. E., Diefenbach, G. J., Anderson, E., &

Meunier, S. A. (2007). Pediatric trichotillomania:

Descriptive psychopathology and an open trial of cognitive behavioral therapy. *Cognitive Behaviour Therapy, 36(3),* 129-144.

Flessner, C. A., Woods, D. W., Franklin, M. E., Keuthen, N. J., Piacentini, J., & Trichotillomania Learning Center-Scientific Advisory Board. (2008). Styles of pulling in youths with trichotillomania: Exploring differences in symptom severity, phenomenology, and comorbid psychiatric symptoms. *Behaviour Research and Therapy,* 46, 1055-1061. doi: 10.1016/j.brat.2008.06.006

Woods, D. W. & Twohig, M. P. (2008). *Treatments that work: Trichotillomania-An ACT-enhanced behavior therapy approach therapist guide.* New York, NY: Oxford University Press.

American Psychiatric Association. *Diagnostic and Statistical Manual of Mental Disorders, 5th ed. (DSM-5). (*American Psychiatric Publishing, Incorporated, 2013).

Christensen, G., Mackenzie, T., & Mitchell, J. *Adult Men And Women With Trichotillomania.* Psychosomatics: 35, 142-169, 1994.

Fux, M., Levine, J., Aviv, A., & Belmaker, R. *Inositol Treatment of Obsessive Compulsive Disorder.* (American Journal of Psychiatry, 1996).

Fred Penzel. *Inositol and Trichotillomania.* (InTouch Magazine, 1997).

Olson, Sheryl, John Bates, and Kathryn Bales. "Early Antecedents of Childhood Impulsivity: The Role of Parent-Child

Interaction, Cognitive Competence, and Temperament." *Journal of Abnormal Child Psychology,* 18.3 (1990): 317-334. Print.

John Khilstrom. "Hypnosis and Cognition." *Psychology of Consciousness: Theory, Research, and Practice,* 1.2 (2014): 139-152. Print.

Flessner CA, Knopik VS, McGeary J. Hair pulling disorder (trichotillomania): genes, neurobiology, and a model for understanding impulsivity and compulsivity. Psychiatry Res. 2012 Apr 24.

Irvin Yalom and Molyn Leszcz. *The Theory and Practice of Group Psychotherapy,* 5th ed. Basic Books, 2005).

# About the Author

Lindsey Marie Muller was born and raised in South Florida. She holds a Master's degree in Clinical/Counseling Psychology, a Master's degree in Clinical Psychology, in addition to three years of doctoral level education. She currently resides in Los Angeles, California where she enjoys the perfect weather, exercising, healthy cooking, sugar-free baking, spas, and meditation. She currently works in private practice. *Life is Trichy* is her first publication.

Made in the USA
Middletown, DE
12 January 2015